Drums of
Change

Books by Janette Oke

Janette Oke's Reflections on the Christmas Story
The Red Geranium

SEASONS OF THE HEART
Once Upon a Summer *Winter Is Not Forever*
The Winds of Autumn *Spring's Gentle Promise*

LOVE COMES SOFTLY
Love Comes Softly *Love's Unending Legacy*
Love's Enduring Promise *Love's Unfolding Dream*
Love's Long Journey *Love Takes Wing*
Love's Abiding Joy *Love Finds a Home*

CANADIAN WEST
When Calls the Heart *When Breaks the Dawn*
When Comes the Spring *When Hope Springs New*

WOMEN OF THE WEST
The Calling of Emily Evans *A Bride for Donnigan*
Julia's Last Hope *Heart of the Wilderness*
Roses for Mama *Too Long a Stranger*
A Woman Named Damaris *The Bluebird and the Sparrow*
They Called Her Mrs. Doc *A Gown of Spanish Lace*
The Measure of a Heart *Drums of Change*

DEVOTIONALS
The Father Who Calls *Father of My Heart*
The Father of Love *Faithful Father*

Janette Oke: A Heart for the Prairie
Biography of Janette Oke by Laurel Oke Logan

The Oke Family Cookbook
by Barbara Oke and Deborah Oke

9601

Janette Oke
Drums of Change

The Story of Running Fawn

BETHANY HOUSE PUBLISHERS
MINNEAPOLIS, MINNESOTA 55438

Cover by Dan Thornberg,
Bethany House Publishers staff artist.

Published by Bethany House Publishers
A Ministry of Bethany Fellowship, Inc.
11300 Hampshire Avenue South
Minneapolis, Minnesota 55438

Printed in the United States of America.

Library of Congress Cataloging-in-Publication Data

Oke, Janette, 1935–
    The drums of change / Janette Oke.
      p. cm.
    ISBN 1–55661–818-2 (cloth).
    ISBN 1–55661–812–3 (pbk.).
    ISBN 1–55661–823–9 (audio book).
    ISBN 1–55661–817–4 (large print).
    1. Indians of North America—Alberta—Fiction. I. Title.
PR9199.3.038D78   1996
813'.54—dc20

                                      96–4436
                                        CIP

In memory of my mother,

Amy Ruggles Steeves,

a godly, loving, woman
who taught us to respect all people
regardless of race or color,
and to show that respect
through an honest concern
for their well-being.

JANETTE OKE was born in Champion, Alberta, during the depression years, to a Canadian prairie farmer and his wife. She is a graduate of Mountain View Bible College in Didsbury, Alberta, where she met her husband, Edward. They were married in May of 1957, and went on to pastor churches in Indiana as well as Calgary and Edmonton, Canada.

The Okes have three sons and one daughter and are enjoying the addition of grandchildren to the family. Edward and Janette have both been active in their local church, serving in various capacities as Sunday-school teachers and board members. They make their home near Calgary, Alberta.

Foreword

This story has grown out of the early history of our province of Alberta. The history timeline will guide the reader through the actual events. The statistics given, the terms of the treaty, and even the words of the two great chiefs at the time of the signing of Treaty Number Seven have been taken from historical accounts. However, the story itself is totally fictional, and as such I have used some liberty in presenting the characters and their lifestyle.

A number of missionaries came west to work among the tribes and to help establish schools. Accounts tell of their suffering along with the Indian people, sharing what little food they had once the buffalo were gone and medicines in times of epidemics. Their dedication deserves recognition, and I have written this story to help deepen our understanding of all whose lives were touched by that period of history with its dramatic time of great change.

Contents

Characters

Running Fawn — young maiden of the Blackfoot Nation, Blackfoot tribe.

Moon Over Trees — her mother

Gray Hawk — her father

Little Brook — sister

Crooked Moose — older brother

Bright Star — younger brother

Calls Through The Night — a tribal chief

Silver Fox — chief's son

Martin Forbes — (Talks With Full Mouth — Man With The Book) — missionary

One With The Wind, Laughing Loon — friends of Running Fawn

Broken Tooth, Stands Alone — Indian boys

Mrs. Nicholson, Miss Brooke, Otis — mission school employees

Historical characters:
Colonel MacLeod (Stamixotokon), *Crowfoot, Red Crow, Medicine Calf, Bull Shield, Louis Riel, Sitting Bull*, and a number of incidental characters.

Historical Chronology of Events

1837   • Smallpox epidemic that wiped out two-thirds of the Blackfoot Nation.

1855   • U.S. tribes signed treaty.

1866   • Trouble in Montana called Blackfoot wars.

1874   • Arrival in the West of the North West Mounted Police.
        • (*Drums of Change* begins.)

1876   • Battle of Little Bighorn between Custer's troops and Sitting Bull.

June   • Alberta Indians petitioned government— concern over number of white settlers.

August   • Treaty Number Six signed with Crees, Assiniboine, and Ojibwas.

1877   • Blackfoot Nation signed Treaty Number Seven at Blackfoot Crossing.
        • Prairie fires drove remaining buffalo herds into Montana.

1878–79 • Tribes followed the buffalo.

1881   • Buffalo gone, tribes straggled back to familiar grounds and many moved to Reserves.

1882   • Blackfoot Reserve divided into North and South Camp. Missions established, along with schools. Some children sent out to larger centers.

1883 • Canadian Pacific Railroad passed through close to the Reserve.

1884 • 234 acres of land under cultivation on Blackfoot Reserve.

1885 • Riel Rebellion
• (*Drums of Change* ends.)

1889 • First coal mine opened by Blackfoot on their Reserve.

1890 • Death of great chief, Crowfoot. Government-appointed Indian agent, located on Reserve, now serving dominant role.

1995 • (October 6, Calgary Herald) Chief Leo Youngman, last surviving direct relative of Chief Crowfoot, passed away at his home on the Siksika Nation Reserve. Youngman traveled to London in 1976 to invite Queen Elizabeth to visit Blackfoot Crossing in 1977 and attend the ceremonies marking the 100th anniversary of the signing of Treaty Number Seven. Prince Charles came in her place.

Chapter One

Her World

The small figure silhouetted against the outcropping of granite stone was not leaning on it but just brushing against it, so she knew it was there. Her gaze took in the full scene before her. A contented sigh escaped into the stillness of the morning and brought a hint of a smile to childish lips. Of all the locations for their camps, this was her favorite. Her most favorite spot in her entire six winters. She loved it. Loved it. She wouldn't have been able to express it in words, but it was more than love. It was a oneness with the surroundings, a oneness she felt in no other place. Like she belonged to the granite rock at her back, to the giant spruce and pine that covered the hillsides, to the call of the loon on the lake to her left, and to the gurgle of the spring that squeezed its crystal water from the rock crevice just up the slope from her. She sighed again, watching her breath in the frosty air, and lifted her face to let the morning sun brush it with gentle fingers of emerging warmth.

It had been a chilly night. She had buried herself in her furs against the cold and snuggled up closely to the back of her older sister. But she could tell today would be fine. Already the sun was making the steam rise from the cold ground and frigid stream water. Today she soon would stop shivering and perhaps even toss aside her heavy woven shawl. Perhaps . . . perhaps there would be many warm days before the deep snows wrapped the camp securely in blankets of winter white. She hoped so. She wanted time to become reacquainted with the place she loved. To wander through the woods and wade in the cold stream. To lie on her back in the tall meadow grasses and watch the vees of geese pass overhead on their way back to their southern homes. To pick the few remaining berries from the wild chokecherry bushes and search for the last remnants of summer wild flowers. She dared to hope there would be many nice fall days remaining, even though the limbs of the birch and poplar were already close to being bare, their summer's green cloaks now spread like rustling gold on the forest paths.

Her eyes took in a nearby poplar whose bare limbs were, for the moment, lavishly decorated with a colorful flock of migrating goldfinches. It was an awesome sight and one that made her heart beat faster. For an instant she imagined joining them and flying off on buoyant wings to wherever they were flying, gaily chattering at one another as they went on their exciting journey—and then she remembered where she was and quickly changed her mind. There was no place in the entire world that she would rather be.

Suddenly she tensed and shifted her body. She lifted her head, tilting it slightly to catch a faint sound that reached her on the gentle wind that played with the loose dark hair against her cheek. She had not, as yet, redone her black braids. She pushed the strands of hair aside with a small, bronze hand so that her full concentration might be given to the sound. Yes. Yes, it was the call of a black bear. Not so much a call as a grunt. Likely a mother, urging her first-year cubs to hurry in their meandering forage for food before they would follow her to the den where she would spend one more winter with them.

She smiled in delight. Wise beyond her years, she knew her people would be very pleased to know that a bear lived close by. Their food supply was assured. If food was scarce in the area, the bear would have moved elsewhere with her growing cubs.

Suddenly she was in a hurry to complete her task and be off. She wanted to tell her family the good news. She would come back to her place for daydreams later. Later when the tasks around the tent home had been completed. Then she would enjoy the pleasures of the warm fall day and dream to her heart's content.

She reached down to retrieve the skin bucket she had placed on the ground at her feet and moved silently forward. The spring was filled with leaves and twigs of the summer months and would need to be cleared again before water could be scooped from the small pool at its base. She was too small to tackle the job herself, and that would be done quickly by one of the young boys. For now she would need only to dip from the flowing stream.

Lightly she hurried back down the trail, her buckskin garments brushing silently against her bare ankles, her moccasins leaving soft feathery imprints in the brown dust of the path. She must get home with the water before her mother came looking for her. She already had earned the reputation of The Dreaming One, a title that she did not carry with honor, for there were many tasks to be done daily in the camp, and it took all hands to care for the needs of the people. She did not wish to be negligent in her duties—she just forgot to be diligent at times. Mother Nature beckoned and called to her. Pleaded with her to come and feast on the beauties and wonders that were spread before her ever-searching eyes.

She had feasted her soul enough for one day, even though she longed to stay and enjoy the return to her favorite camp.

But her mother would be waiting for the water, and her father would be pleased to hear that a bear shared their mountainside.

❦   ❦   ❦

Her mother lifted her face from the fire she was tending with small dry sticks. There was a hint of reproof in her dark eyes, but she did not raise her voice. In fact, it was several minutes before the woman spoke at all.

The heavy kettle, purchased with beaver pelts from trappers who passed through the area, balanced on three stones over the dancing flames and now held the water from the stream. Already the bannock was cooking. Just looking at it made the little girl's stomach rumble in anticipation.

"I think we will make a name change," said the mother in the soft tones of their simple native tongue.

The girl frowned.

The mother did not look up from her task.

"Your father calls you Running Fawn. I think we should call you Three-leg Porcupine."

She knew her mother was teasing, yet there was enough truth to the comment to make her cheeks warm. With all four legs in good condition, a porcupine was the slowest creature of the forest. A three-legged porcupine would be slow indeed.

But her mother quickly changed the topic of discussion. "Is the spring good?"

It was a question of great importance. They needed the spring.

"Yes." She could not keep the enthusiasm from her voice. Her dark eyes had an even brighter sparkle. "And I heard a black bear—calling to her cubs," she hurried on, happy that she was the one to first discover such an important fact.

Her mother lifted her face, her own eyes reflecting the sparkle of the young girl's.

"That is good," she said with a nod, almost as though she was now commending her daughter for lingering in the woods to bring the good news. "That is good," she said again, turning back to the bannock.

"Shall I tell Father?" asked the child eagerly.

"He is with the horses," replied her mother. "Will be here soon. And hungry."

"And Crooked Moose?"

"With Father."

Running Fawn shifted lightly from one foot to the other.

She was impatient to share her exciting information about the bear with someone else. Maybe her older sister.

"Little Brook?" she inquired.

"Gathering wood for fire," replied her mother without lifting her eyes or her voice.

There was silence for a few moments. Running Fawn shifted her weight again. Her mother did raise her eyes then. She even smiled her quiet smile.

"You run," she said good-naturedly. "Tell of bear."

Running Fawn did not stop to daydream or dawdle. On swift feet she ran toward the meadow where the horses were grazed.

Her mother looked after her and shook her head as she chuckled softly. The young girl was now living up to her name. Perhaps they would not need to change it after all.

❧   ❧   ❧

During the daylight hours, the weather remained warm and sunny long enough for the camp to be well settled before winter began. There were many things that needed to be done so the people would be ready for the cold and snow. The work proceeded rapidly with every able pair of hands assuming the various tasks. Running Fawn felt as though she spent all her days on the path that led to the spring, carrying pail after pail of water for her mother's use. It turned out that she had little time to dream or to bask in the color of the pleasant fall. Every day the calls of the geese and the persistent tugging of the brisk autumn wind reminded them that time for winter stores was soon coming to an end.

The hunters had verified Running Fawn's report that they shared their area with a mother black bear and two healthy cubs. The news brought much chatter around the campfires. It was the first time a bear had been seen at this location in the last three years. A fact that had been causing concern among the elders. They feared that their sure food supply was threatened and that wintering in the area might bring hardship to the group. But now with the presence of the mother and her offspring, who were still feeding on nearby grubs and leftover berries, the camp was in an almost jovial mood. Daily hunting parties went out and most often returned with game to be roasted over open fires or dried for future use.

For Running Fawn the bear was more than good news. It was a wondrous reprieve. She had heard talk around the campfires indicating the possibility that this campsite no longer was able to meet the needs of the small band. The chief had even talked of searching for a different site when the camp moved from the summer grazing ground. Running Fawn had been stricken when she heard the words. Her favorite spot. Not to see it again. She had wept silently when she went to her blankets that night, fighting to keep her sobs from waking her older sister.

It was true that all the land was "good." But this place— this place where she had first opened her eyes to look out upon a new world, this place of her birth, was especially dear to her heart. She had spent every one of her six winters in this camp. She couldn't imagine life without it.

꙳   ꙳   ꙳

With the small clearing near the spring occupied by a cluster of scattered tent homes, the bear moved her cubs a short distance downstream. Many times a day she lifted her long, sharp nose to check the wind for threatening scents. She carefully scanned a meadow before every appearance from the bush. Daily she grew a bit more nervous, a little more cautious, and coaxed her adventuresome cubs to stay a little closer to her side. They had grown well on the abundance of summer and were less attentive to her voice, so her patience was often worn thin, and an occasional cuff sent one or the other crying out in pain or rage. They could not understand the change in her behavior.

Had the mother known, she would have relaxed her vigil.

The nearby tents with their chattering occupants posed no threat to her existence. Indeed, they would have been willing to guard her against other intruders. She was a good omen. A "sister" in the wild. They kept their distance but read her signs and movements as thoroughly as one might read a book. The time when she would decide to forsake her feeding and retire to her den for the winter would give them indication of the kind of winter they too would face.

The evenings were becoming increasingly chilly, and the she-bear had the urge to seek out a safe den and curl up with her growing cubs. But something drove her on, feeding and foraging for her cubs and adding more fat to the already thick layer that would be their winter insulation and nourishment. That, too, was noted.

"Long winter," voiced one of the hunters around the evening fire. "Mother Bear still feeds. Squirrels still store. Even on cold days. Rabbit has long, thick fur. Long winter."

Others nodded.

"Birds all go," observed another, his weathered face proclaiming that he had watched many winters come and go and thus was authorized to speak. "Beavers build high dam. They want deep water."

Faces sobered and daylight activity increased. All signs led to a long, cold winter, and once it arrived there would be little the camp could do to increase the food supply. Their time would be taken with finding enough wood to keep the tepee fires going.

☙ ☙ ☙

True to prediction, the cold north winds drove Old Man Winter into the area. The sharp sting of the storm soon had the horses in the meadow bunched together, heads down, backs to the wind. The few leaves stubbornly clinging to the poplar and birch trees were soon off on a twisting, reeling journey, helpless against the strength of the current that snatched them from the branches.

Running Fawn was sent along with Little Brook to hurriedly gather an armload of wood for the inside fire. There no longer would be any fire built outside of the tepee. Every scrap of wood and hint of warmth was hoarded. The season of stinging eyes and huddling in furry robes was once again upon them.

Running Fawn was thankful she had been born a girl child. She would not need to hunt in the cold or care for horses that unreasonably resisted attempts to ease their discomfort by tethering them close to the sheltering trees.

She did have to venture out for water from the ice-covered stream. The spring would now be locked away behind ice and snow until warm weather returned to release it from winter's grip. And she had to help Little Brook with the gathering of firewood. On the coldest days the task would not be an easy one, but it would be a chance to look out at the world she loved in its new white dress.

But for the most part, she would be happy to remain in the tent, close to the warmth of the fire, adjusting her stinging eyes to the dim light so she might help with the sewing. Or squatting before the fire as she stirred the cooking pot, head turned slightly away from the smoke that always eventually made tears trickle down her soft, dark cheeks.

Running Fawn felt only contentment. She had no concerns for her future or her safety as she listened, in welcoming silence, as the north wind, day after day, tore at the tent poles and piled the heavy, white blanket of snow against the walls of the tent skins.

Chapter Two

The Decision

"What do you think?"

"He's young."

The gray-haired man at the head of the table seemed to reflect on the words for some minutes as he gently stroked the trimmed beard that covered his chin. "Yes," he agreed at length. "Very young."

"But he has passion," put in the man in the dark brown suit as he turned to the elderly chairman. He spoke the words with exuberance, force, as though he too had passion.

The gray head nodded and the owner lifted up his face, revealing the spark in his steely blue eyes. Though an old man, his face still reflected a passion of its own.

"He certainly knows the Scriptures," interjected a man with horn-rimmed glasses, obviously the scholar of the group, and his words denoted that he felt strongly concerning the need for such knowledge.

"He *is* young," the chairman mused aloud, leaning back in his chair and making a bridge with his long, tapering fingers.

"Even for someone older—more experienced—it will not be an easy task," spoke the man to his left. He was a rather rotund person with a full face that appeared to want to smile and found it hard to show the proper solemnity for this serious occasion.

"No," agreed the chairman. "No, it will not be an easy task."

His bridge played a little tattoo as the fingers parted and came back together again and again like the soft, distant rhythm of beating drums.

The other man at the table cleared his throat in preparation to speak. He seemed hesitant to even ask the question. "Why—" His voice still objected to being heard. He cleared his throat again. "Why the—Territory Indians?" he managed to say through his constricted throat.

Four pairs of eyes turned to the questioner. For one moment he looked like he wished to withdraw the query. Then the drumming fingers stilled, and the chairman leaned forward and fixed blue eyes on the speaker.

"I asked him that very question myself," he said, and the others turned their full attention back to him.

He stopped to shuffle a few papers before he went on to answer. When he spoke again, his eyes glistened with unshed tears.

"He has—a real—burden, if you will. An intense love. A desire to take to them the Gospel."

He blinked as though to rid himself of the unwanted tears, then looked evenly at the four men about the table. "It's genuine. I could sense it. He made me . . . made me long to be young again so that I, too, might go. I have never seen such—intensity."

"But he hasn't even met the—"

"No—there you are wrong. He grew up in the West—until the age of ten. At that time he lost his father, and his mother moved back to the East. But he knew them—as a child. Played with the Indian boys. His father ran a local Post. Used to trade them knives and guns and cooking pots—for furs. He knows them all right. He's been—longing to get back to them. It's been the sole purpose in his training—his preparation. To go back."

"I didn't know," someone whispered and others nodded

their agreement. It seemed that the new knowledge would affect the decision to be made.

They sat in a few moments of silence while they thought about the young man's "call." At last the man in the brown suit spoke.

"So what is he proposing?"

"He wishes to go as soon as we can send him."

"And that will be?" asked the bespectacled man.

"Well, certainly not now—with winter closing in. Perhaps first thing in the spring. I know he's chafing to be on his way. But it isn't even practical to expect to cross the prairies at this time of year. And there will be much to be done to prepare for the journey. In the spring, I'd say. Even that will not be easy travel."

"And he'll go—?"

"By boat mostly. He said he is sure he can find some Hudson's Bay trappers going west. He's willing to travel with them. Says that will be the cheapest and most assured way. I think that's the way he and his mother made their way back east."

Heads nodded. "If he can do that, it would certainly be the most practical," agreed the brown-suited man.

"What are his plans?"

"He wants to get established with a local tribe. Prove he is coming as a friend. There is still a bit of mistrust there. More . . . hesitation than hostility. But he feels it will take a bit of time for them to accept him—and his God."

Heads nodded again.

"He is most anxious to start a school. Feels that if he really is to make an impact on their lives, he must train their young so they can read the Scriptures for themselves."

"That will be a slow business," said the scholar, "even though most necessary. I understand that none of the tribes have their language in written form."

"He will teach them English," responded the gray-haired man.

"English? Then he certainly will need a school. Does he

think they will allow their children to attend?"

"It will take dedication—and diligence—to make them understand that it is for their good. He will need to win the confidence of the elders in order for the task to be accomplished."

"And he thinks he can?"

It was a candid, direct question. Terse, but intent. On this fact the whole mission was dependent.

The older man nodded and his eyes misted again. "He has such a—love—such a passion—that he sees no reason why they shouldn't respond to him in kind. He keeps . . . keeps repeating Scripture verses that promise him the Lord's presence—that promise the victory, through Christ Jesus. Oh, he has no doubt that his mission will be successful."

Each showing the emotion of the moment in different ways, five pairs of eyes looked down at five pairs of folded hands. The jolly man spoke and this time his voice held the proper solemnity for the serious occasion. "Then I think we should send him—with our prayers and blessing," he said, and four voices followed his words with a soft but heartfelt "Amen."

It was decided. The Mission Society would ordain and send forth the young Reverend Martin Forbes as soon as the spring thaws deemed the land fit for travel.

☙   ☙   ☙

The long, cold winter would have been a harsh one had not the tribe had plenty of warning and been diligent in their preparation. Mother Earth had cooperated in sending game back to the winter campsite. Remarks were heard around campfires about the blessing bestowed upon them and their thankful response to the spirit in charge of their well-being.

Running Fawn pondered the comments. She too felt thankfulness, but in her youthful innocence she wondered what had brought about the change. Had they been extra good or extra wise over the months of the past summer? Had they been bad the years before? Why was Mother Earth and the great Sun God smiling on them again, even in the midst of the cold darkness of winter? Why was the strength of the North Wind not able to penetrate the walls of the tents no matter how fiercely it blew? Why was game found where none had been in previous years so that the cooking pots were never empty or stomachs pained with hunger? What was the secret of plenty, and how could they guard it for the future?

Whenever Running Fawn approached her mother with one of her puzzling concerns, Moon Over Trees shrugged off the question and cast a glance nervously about the tepee. "Do not question the gods," she cautioned. "Do not make them angry. Someday, when you have a spiritual journey, they may tell you in vision. Maybe not. For now—walk with head bowed."

So Running Fawn buried her questions. Or at least she tried. But they stayed in the back of her mind to haunt her.

꘎   ꘎   ꘎

To the impatient young man who paced back and forth in his small one-room apartment, it seemed that spring would never come. He had been accepted by the Mission Board, and had made his arrangement with the three trappers who would be traveling west as soon as the spring thaws freed the rivers from their wintry, icy grip. He had purchased and stored his supplies for the long trip. He had his plans in place, his destination well in mind. But winter dragged on and on.

He tried hard to fill his days with practical things. Studying the Scriptures, memorization, mapping out his plans carefully on sheets of precious paper from his scant supplies. He walked the streets to encourage those in need, preached on the street corners, established a local prayer group, and shared his daily bread with those less fortunate. Yet he still longed to be off on the journey that would take him west.

Longed to start the mission work that he had trained himself for. Each storm that blew through the area, each new scattering of snow and sweep of frigid wind, made his impatience more evident. Would spring never come?

But at last it did—as it always must. And with a great deal of enthusiasm, he carted his carefully chosen stores over to the small local wharf and joined his travel-mates in loading the canoes until they were low in the water. They would become lighter and lighter as they traveled, for many of the supplies would be used en route. And, undoubtedly, even when one tried to guard against it, they would have their losses to river, rapids, thieves or elements. He prayed that his Bible and other books might be spared. He would rather go without food.

Yes, their physical loads would lessen, but his spiritual burden, his great desire, would only grow and grow as they paddled the many miles that would take them to the West.

꙳   ꙳   ꙳

Standing at the base of the spring, Running Fawn gazed with mixed emotions at a small stream bubbling to the surface through cracks in the ice and snow. Spring was coming. She could not but be glad to be released once more from winter's deep chill, yet the return of warm weather would soon mean that the people would be breaking camp and traveling to the plains to a summer campsite.

Already she had spotted returning crows and watched as geese honked their winged way northward overhead. The banks of snow were receding along the path to the stream, and the rabbits were slowly getting back some tinges of summer brown on their fur.

But it was the water that was the sure sign winter was leaving the area. When the spring began to bubble, and then to flow, winter had surely lost its grip on the land.

Though it had been a long winter, it had not been a particularly difficult one. Still, the mood of the camp lightened with the promise of another summer. Women left the comfort of their tents and called to one another as they cooked over outside campfires, glad to stretch their legs and rest their eyes. Young boys challenged one another to games of skill while young girls shyly watched. Older folks were helped to a place in the midday sun so that arthritic bones could be warmed from winter's chill. But it was the men of the tribe who reacted with the most enthusiasm. The long days of winter had mostly shut them in, except for the occasional hunting parties that brought in the fresh meat or the trappers who worked over the pelts of beaver or fox. The young men in particular were relieved to be more freely around and about again. Voices filled the air as they challenged one another to mount the horses that had been idly feeding over the winter months, or tested their bows to see if their arrows still flew with swiftness and accuracy.

Running Fawn loved the springtime. Yet she did wish they could forget about the move to the plains and just stay on where they were. It was a perfect place. The wild game had lasted well through the winter months. There was meat for the cooking pots. The spring waters were flowing again. They were secluded, almost hidden from the rest of the world. On the plains would be many people. Some viewed as old friends. Many others as a part of their great Blackfoot Nation. A few known as longtime enemies. But now . . . now there were also those who were strangers. They were the ones who disturbed her, even as they roused her curiosity.

They were white of skin and wore strange clothes and talked a strange language and had strange ways of doing things. There was much discussion around the campfires about these people. Some saw them as intruders, a threat to the supply of beaver or buffalo. Others saw them as curiosity pieces, amusing and harmless, unable to withstand the harshness of the new land. There were those who saw them as an advantage, for they brought with them pots and blankets and bright knives with shiny sharp blades. These foolish white men bartered those treasures for a mere pelt or two—and pelts were plentiful.

But already the people had come to realize that there were good and bad among these strangers. Some were willing to live by the code of the land, others seemed intent upon destroying everything in their wake as they swept their way westward. Some were silent in their approach into the Indian's world. Others noisily thundered their way across the prairies, shooting their loud guns and chopping at trees with angry sticks fastened with sharp blades that rang out in the stillness and flashed brilliantly in the sunlight.

Many of the women were deathly afraid of the white men. And children, driven by fear of the unknown, often ran to hide among the bushes, then peered out from cover, curiosity overcoming their good judgment.

Moon Over Trees, Running Fawn's mother, was not terrified by the white newcomers, but she did still favor a bit of caution. They liked her beadwork and paid her well in pots and trinkets, but she was careful to always be in the company of her husband and son when she did her bartering, and she cautioned her daughters, with dark glances from her knowing eyes, to stay within the circle of the family.

So part of Running Fawn wished that spring had not come, even as she exulted in the fact that it had surely arrived. She didn't like the thought of breaking up camp and heading out into the larger world. She didn't like change. She longed for things to stay just as they were.

Chapter Three

Summer Camp

They began their journey on a warm spring day. Already the early flowers were poking from the ground, and birds were calling excitedly from the limbs of newly leafed branches, eager to get at the task of building the yearly nest.

The tent skins had been removed and the tent poles lowered. Cooking pots and bedding were bundled and stacked on the backs of pack animals or arranged on travois. Old people and small children settled among the blankets and rolls, and the long procession began to move out from the small meadow where they had been securely tucked for the winter months.

Horses, too long allowed freedom from burdens, were frisky and skittish as they were pressed back into service. Running Fawn knew that after a few days on the trail they would settle into a more sensible frame of mind.

She sighed and hoisted the small bundle that was hers to carry. She joined a small group of chattering girls, far more eager than she to be on the trail that would take them over many miles, away from the tucked-in arms of her beloved Rocky Mountain Valley, to the wide sweeps of the open plains. A trail that would take many days and result in aching backs and tired feet. But a trail that would join them together with many of their own people, people scattered over the vastness of the land in smaller bands. People who shared their tongue, their nomadic way of life, and their intense religion. Running Fawn knew that she should feel the excitement the others evidenced, but she could feel only sorrow. She would miss their winter camping grounds, the place of her birth. It would be such a long time until she saw it again.

Her heart heavy, her eyes fixed straight ahead, she found a place in the line of young girls. Though every part of her being longed to turn and run back to the familiar site, she lifted a stubborn chin, shifted her little pack more securely, and refused to glance back even for one final look.

❧ ❧ ❧

The letter arrived near the end of October. The first communication from the Reverend Martin Forbes brought a sigh of relief from those who received it. It had been a long time since the young man set out for the West. It began,

August 14, 1875

Gentlemen and Esteemed Brothers,

I have reached the "Land of Promise" after a difficult and arduous journey. We had many obstacles to overcome. Twice we were capsized in the river rapids. One canoe of supplies was totally lost to a band of marauders. Severe dysentery kept us confined to our camp for ten days. Swarms of mosquitoes and blackflies threatened to overtake us. We nearly lost one of our fellow travelers by drowning. But God was good and we are now safely on the plains.

I have been welcomed at the fort manned by the North West Mounted Police. They do not claim to share my religious concern for the Indian nation but have been kind and courteous nonetheless. I have been advised that I may stay and rest and recuperate until such time as I feel fit to move on.

My first endeavor will be to scout out the area and discover just what will be the most advantageous approach in reaching out to the people. I will also begin to learn the language of the Blackfoot tribe. I covet your prayers as I seek the direction of Almighty God.

I will report again as soon as I have further news.

> Yours in His service,
> Martin D. Forbes,
> Minister of the Gospel

A collective sigh followed the reading of the letter. Then heads bowed as the chairman of the Missions Board led the group in prayer for the young man out on the western plains.

☙　　☙　　☙

Even Running Fawn felt the excitement as the straggling little band came in sight of the large camp. The tents of the Blackfoot tribe stretched along the banks of the Bow River at the place known as Blackfoot Crossing. Many had arrived there before them. Such meetings of the whole nation were always charged with energy, filled with days of feasting, games, and dancing—all interlaced with lengthy discussions by chiefs, great and small, and liberally sprinkled with solemn religious ceremonies.

Running Fawn knew the younger ones would be invited to share in only a few of the major events, but she still would hear scatterings of talk and sense the pulse of her people. She and the others her age would be allowed to feast and to dance and to watch some of the ceremonies as the leaders performed the religious rites. That was exciting. And she would be able to become reacquainted with young girls from the other bands.

Even though their numbers had been depleted by the smallpox epidemic that had swept through the land before she was born, the size and strength of the nation filled her with awe and pride. The Blackfoot were a great people, just as her father and mother were constantly reminding her.

Yet it was a bit frightening, too. There were so many she did not know, so many important elders. For a shy six-year-old from a small band it was almost overwhelming. She was tempted to bury her face in her mother's long skirts and cling to her for safety and assurance.

Little Brook did not seem to share her concern. Already Running Fawn's sister was dashing ahead with a group of older girls, shouting to a welcoming committee of girls their age who were running to meet them. Running Fawn did not even recognize any of the faces.

She cast a glance around for reassurance that her mother was not far away and gradually retreated from the little group with whom she walked. Slowly, so as not to be conspicuous, she eased into her mother's circle of chattering women.

Her friends did not seem to miss her as they hurried on to mix with children from the other bands.

Running Fawn fell into step just behind her mother. She longed to reach out and grab a handful of the shawl's fringe that fluttered softly in the prairie wind, but she held back. She was no longer an infant, even though she was the youngest member of the family. At least for the present. Her mother was with child again and excited over the fact. Running Fawn was uncertain as to her own feelings. She knew that her mother had already lost four children and had three that lived. It was not a bad average for a mother in the band. But this new child could even the tally. That would be better than average. Moon Over Trees fervently hoped to make her husband proud by bearing him four living children, and Running Fawn knew her mother longed for the new baby to be a son. Watching her mother grow big with child caused fear to gnaw away at the insides of the small girl. Once the new baby was born, what would be her place, her position, in the family circle? She had the feeling that she would never be able to reach for her mother again. The thought made a strange coldness in her chest, even though the noonday sun was hot in the prairie sky.

❦   ❦   ❦

The days of feasting and merrymaking began each morning soon after the rising of the sun and carried on until long after the moon had risen at night. There was much talking and visiting from lodge to lodge. Frequent gatherings around a neighbor's fire. Many contests to test the young braves' skills, while onlookers noisily expressed opinions over the outcome. There were a few squabbles and evidence of long-carried grudges, when chiefs had to intervene and settle down hotheaded young men. But for the most part the days passed without major incidents. Running Fawn was even beginning to feel that she could fit in with this large mass of people.

She was assigned her usual duty of water carrier and spent many hours on the dusty trail that led to the riverbank.

But this trail was not good for dreaming. It was always busy with other young girls, water buckets in hand, as they too provided water for their families. Chattering boys crowded the pathway as they made their way to the river for an afternoon swim, and womenfolk or older girls, laundry bundles in hand, also shared the trail. There was no time for Running Fawn to stop and feel the gentleness of the quiet. The air was filled with noise and motion and the smoke of many fires. Running Fawn often longed for the quiet and peace of their mountain camp where she could feel at one with the openness, the solitude, the vastness of the sweeping hills around her.

※   ※   ※

Ten days into the festivities a meeting of chiefs and important elders was held in the Sweat Lodge. Running Fawn had taken no particular interest in the meeting. The men of the tribe were always holding powwows that seemed to have little bearing on her life. But she could not help but hear the talk as the women chatted about the open fires. There was something different about this meeting. Something stirring the blood of everyone in the camp. Running Fawn, curious and a little frightened, found herself easing toward the group of women rather than running to play with the other girls her age.

Over and over the discussion made reference to the white man. Running Fawn found herself shivering every time the words were mentioned.

"Too many. Too many have come," said an elderly woman as she stirred a large pot of venison stew.

"Some are good." The comment came from Moon Over Trees, Running Fawn's mother.

"Some are bad," said an old woman with a seamed, weathered face. She spat in the dust to accentuate her words. "Bring death. Sickness. Whiskey. Bring death." She spat again.

"Too many," reiterated the first speaker. "Too many. Take too many buffalo."

Moon Over Trees nodded. It was true. The buffalo were getting more scarce. But, still, there were many of the large beasts feeding on the grassy plains. She was not worried.

"Some good," she said again. "The Red Coat are good."

There were many nods about the fire. One young maiden dropped her eyes and even blushed at the mention of the North West Mounted Police in their scarlet coats. Running Fawn puzzled over the flushed cheeks.

"I like their trade," said a smaller woman whom Running Fawn did not know. "They like beadwork. They pay good."

Many nodded. It was true. Their life had become much easier since the trading fort had been established.

"Too many," insisted the first woman. "Too many have come. They never stop. They come and come. You will see."

It was an ominous thought. Running Fawn shivered again and drew back into the shadows. She did not wish to hear any more.

The second report arrived a short two weeks after the first had been received.

Dear Christian Brothers,

After several trips out into the country round about, I still am uncertain as to where I am to begin my work. The Indian people are, for the most part, quite open and accepting. I have felt no hostility. In fact they have been courteous and hospitable. On several occasions I have been invited to share a meal and even a tent. For this I thank the Lord, and I thank you for your prayers.

There are some concerns. As you know, the whiskey traders caused much trouble in the area a few years back. Thank God, due to the North West Mounted Police, that problem has now been dealt with. But the aftereffects have remained. Many of the Indian people have discovered strong drink to be to their liking and seek ways to get the bootleg whiskey from other sources. This is of great concern to the North West Mounted Police force, as it is to us all. Many have succumbed to the ill effects of the illegal liquor. In one winter alone, seventy members of the noble Bloods, a division of the Blackfoots, were killed in drunken quarrels at just one of the posts. Others, poisoned by the evil brew, were frozen to death while intoxicated or shot over altercations caused by the evil trade.

Although the trading centers that promoted the transactions in illegal whiskey have been cleaned up, I fear that the effects will be with the people for years to come.

There is also much concern regarding diseases that have come to the area with the white man. In 1837–38, two thirds of the Blackfoot Nation was wiped out in a smallpox epidemic. Since that time many others have died from various diseases, though never to that great extent again. But each year more lives are lost. We have no way to bring medicines or treatment to the people. It causes me much grief to hear of the great losses. It is little wonder that some of the chiefs are concerned regarding the great influx of settlers and trades people. Please pray that the door will not be closed even before we have a chance to influence them for Christ. Already rumblings are reaching us from south of the border, and we feel that the Canadian tribes might be greatly influenced by the unrest.

I do covet your earnest prayers.

In His service,
Martin D. Forbes,
Minister of Christ

⚜   ⚜   ⚜

Running Fawn awoke to the beating of the drums. There was something different about the rhythm. Something strange about the intensity. Something challenging in the tone of the voices that offered the chants. She shivered in her blankets, even though the night was still warm. She stirred and moved to crowd closer to Little Brook. But the shared pallet was empty of her sister. She was alone. She called out softly in the darkness, seeking some assurance from her mother. There was no answer to her cry.

Frightened, she pushed the blanket aside and crawled across the hard dirt floor on all fours. She felt her mother's bed. There was no one there. Heart pounding, she crawled the rest of the way to the opening of the tent and pushed back the heavy flap. In the sky she could see the reflection of the fire. It was larger than a cooking fire would be. Even brighter than the usual communal fire. She could hear the drums plainly now, and the earth beneath her reverberated with the beating of many feet against the hard-packed ground. The voices rose and fell with a strange eeriness that made her spine tingle and her hair pull at the base of her neck. She wanted to crawl back into her blankets and bury her head, but she could not bear to be alone.

She ran the short distance toward the fire, her heart pounding even harder within her chest. An enormous group of people spilled out over the prairie. She had never seen such a large gathering all in one place. Even the women, sitting on the sidelines with blankets wrapped around their shoulders, sang and swayed as the drums beat and the men danced and the feet continued to thump thump thump against the trembling ground.

Running Fawn looked around the gathering with wild eyes. She would never find her mother in such a press of people.

And then she spotted Little Brook and some of the fear left her. At least her sister was there. Her sister would know where their mother was.

Running Fawn pushed through the cluster of young girls until she was able to reach out and tug at Little Brook's long shawl.

"Where is Mother?" she questioned loudly. The thundering of the drums made it hard to be heard.

Little Brook turned. Her eyes widened as they acknowledged her younger sister, but it was clear she had not heard the girl's words.

"Where is Mother?" Running Fawn shouted again, fear making her voice break.

Little Brook just gave a careless shrug of her shoulders and waved a hand toward a large group of women.

Running Fawn's heart again thudded with fear. She would never find her. Never. Not in the tangle of swaying bodies and waving shawls. With a look of despair she pushed herself forward until she was close to Little Brook's side and stubbornly took her position. She reached out one small hand and gathered folds of Little Brook's shawl in a tightened fist, determined to hang on despite whatever came. She would not find herself alone again.

"What happened?" she asked Little Brook, with a sharp tug at the shawl.

Little Brook's eyes were shining with excitement, reflected by the bright full moon overhead.

"The chiefs have spoken," she said hoarsely.

"What? What have they spoken?"

"They are going to the White Fort. They are in agreement. They wish to stop the many white men from coming to our land."

Running Fawn let the breath ease from her body. Some of the tension began to seep away from her. Her small shoulders drooped in relieved acceptance. There was nothing wrong. The chiefs were taking care of the people. They were restoring their world to what it had always been. From now on she would not need to feel terror at the change any longer.

Chapter Four

1876–1877

Running Fawn was feeling impatient. It seemed long past time for the large camp to break up and for the bands to go their separate ways. But the people appeared reluctant to leave the massive campsite. Night after night the drums beat out their song of unity, yet with its underlying note of discord. Daily the talk around the campfire centered on the interests of the people. The delegation had been dispatched to speak with the Great White Fathers, who gave them audience and expressed some appreciation for their concerns. But no real solution was evident.

"The Great White Mother, the Queen of England, cares for her people," the delegation was assured. The words were brought back to the camp to be deliberated and measured and debated. Some found comfort, others doubted.

Around the campfires and in the Sweat Lodges, the word "treaty" was often heard. Running Fawn had no idea what the word meant. She did know that it brought various responses. Her father spoke against the idea. After all, the brothers across the border had signed a treaty in 1855. The white man had not honored the treaty but had broken it over and over again. What good would a treaty do the people?

Their own band's chief, Calls Through The Night, was also against the idea of signing a treaty. It would only bring more white settlers to the area and more renegade Indians who would infringe upon their hunting grounds, further deplete the buffalo, and make raids on their herds of horses.

But the great chief of the whole Blackfoot tribe, Chief Crowfoot, was not ready to condemn the idea of signing. He had visited the great fort on the open plains and had seen firsthand the large contingent of white soldiers, all carrying weapons of war. He knew that his people would never be able to stand against them. Wisdom of years and experience told him that it would be better to sign than to condemn his people to certain death.

Running Fawn felt confused and unsettled by the talk. The uncertainty. She longed to return to the safety of their own hills.

Eventually small bands began to separate themselves from the main body and ride off to make their own camps where the hunting grounds would not need to be shared with such a large body of people.

But when the time came that Calls Through The Night decided his little band would leave the gathering, they did not head for the familiar hills closer to the mountains. He had decided to stay in a sheltered valley along the Bow River not many miles upstream from the large camp. Running Fawn was disappointed and frightened by this decision. Why did he wish to remain on the open plain? Why had they not moved back toward the western hills and her favorite place in the whole world? Surely there was some mistake.

But her small voice would not be heard against the loud voices of the elders, she knew that. So she buried her thoughts and fears and stayed as close to her mother's campfire as she was able.

✢   ✢   ✢

They had not been at the new camp for long when they had a visitor. The man was a member of the Blood tribe, a part of the Blackfoot Nation. Running Fawn watched him arrive and be properly received by Chief Calls Through The

Night. The two disappeared into the chief's tent, and soon other elders were gathering around the chief's fire.

Word drifted from the very folds of the tent skins and was soon being whispered around campfires by women bending over their cooking pots.

There was to be an uprising. The great Chief Sitting Bull to the south was tired of the broken promises and the intrusion of settlers and soldiers. He was going to settle the issue of land once and for all and was asking his brothers north of the border to join him. The invitation had been delivered to Chief Crowfoot. He was to make a decision. How many chiefs would join him if he chose to go?

Long into the night the council fires burned. In the early morning light many of the elders mounted their horses and followed Chief Calls Through The Night out of the camp in the company of the Blood warrior.

Running Fawn had never felt so frightened. Among the men who rode off at the first light of dawn was her father. She knew little of uprisings, nothing of treaties, but she did know of wars and raids. There were always horses that returned with no riders. There was always much weeping and wailing within the camp as the women mourned their dead, and there was always loud beating of the drums and display of weapons and bravado as the braves voiced their intent for revenge.

The tension in the camp grew as the days slowly passed. Running Fawn could feel it. Could hear it in the muted voices. Could sense it in the tightness of her mother's jaw as she worked at the scraping of the buffalo hides.

"When will he be back?" she dared to ask one day.

She did not speak her father's name, but she knew her mother would understand her meaning.

"When he is finished," her mother responded and turned her eyes back to the skin.

Running Fawn saw how tense her mother was, could see it in the movement of her brown hands.

She had to ask. Had to know. "Will it take long—to drive away the Whites?"

"Perhaps," said her mother.

"Why did they come?"

"Because what we have is good."

Running Fawn let her eyes drift over the wide open prairie with its wind-browned grasses and its distant hills, smoky blue in the gathering twilight. She longed for the far-off mountains, too far away to even be seen, yet inwardly she could hear their call, sense their presence. Yes. What they had was good. No wonder the pale-faced people wanted to take it from them.

She hoped her father and the other brave warriors of her people would be able to stop them—soon.

❧   ❧   ❧

They did not need to wait or wonder for many more days. A cloud of dust rising on the open prairie meant that a group of riders was coming their way. At first there was concern bordering on fear. But as the riders drew nearer the small band realized that it was indeed their own men who were returning to camp. The concern turned to joy. It had not taken long for the nation to defeat the enemy.

Each woman left her tanning rack or cooking pot with grateful cries yet a fearful heart. Would her warrior be one that was missing?

But as they drew nearer to the returning party there was great rejoicing. Not one pony was without a rider. Cries of thankfulness lifted upward. They had been victorious. They had won the battle quickly, without a single loss.

There was both surprise and a measure of disappointment when they learned the whole truth. There had been no participation in the uprising. The great Chief Crowfoot had declined Sitting Bull's invitation. "We can never stop their guns," he tried to reason. "They come, more and more."

Many of the young braves had been anxious to be involved. Their hot blood cried for action against the intruders. If they didn't fight, how would they survive?

Running Fawn was puzzled by the whole proceeding. Why didn't they just go back to their hills and live as they always had? Why did the elders think they had to do anything differently than they always had? Why did there have to be change?

December 5, 1876

Dear Brothers in Christ,

I have been visiting many of the small bands camped around the southern territories. But now the weather has grown bitterly cold, and I fear that I may be shut in until spring.

This has been a troubling year. Sitting Bull and his people accomplished a great feat, from the Indian's standpoint. He and his remaining band are now holed up in the Cyprus Hills. The North West Mounted Police are intent on getting them back south to their own side of the border as the law does not allow fugitives from justice to be harbored. Personally I feel great compassion for them. I tried to get permission to visit their camp but was refused. Their presence here has caused much tension among the tribes of the Canadian plains. It did not help when the Northern Indians signed a treaty in August. Many others saw it as giving in to the demands of the whites. Perhaps even Sitting Bull's short-lived victory has made them realize that they will never be the winners in the situation.

This is a great time of change for the Indian people and things will continue to get worse. I long to share the Gospel with them, for I fear that the only way they will make it through the dark years ahead is with the help of God. May He grant us wisdom in our dealings with them.

I do wish you and your families a blessed and joyous

Christmas season. May the presence of the Christ of Christmas warm your hearts and fill your being.

Sincerely in Him,
Martin D. Forbes,
Minister of Our Lord

❧   ❧   ❧

When spring finally came again, Running Fawn welcomed it, even though it was not the same as it had always been at their former winter camp. It turned out that the chief had not returned his band to the shelter of the Rockies and the spot Running Fawn loved. The small girl had mourned silently as they had settled into the camp in the draw near the Bow River, but she knew there would be no advantage in protesting. The chief knew what was best for his people.

As the first crocuses began to appear on the bare, brown hills, her heart began to sing again. She felt that she was finally released from the heavy burden that was far more than the snows of winter, though she could not have put into words the heaviness that had troubled her heart.

Through the summer months the band became nomadic, following the herds of buffalo that still dotted the prairie. There was talk about the lessening of the great numbers, but when they went on the hunt, there were still a multitude of animals to be quickly skinned and hides that would later be tanned. Running Fawn saw no cause for alarm and her mother seemed to share her feelings.

Over the winter months the new baby had arrived—a boy. Her mother had offered her thanks to the Sun God in appreciation. The baby seemed healthy, and even Running Fawn could not resist the smiles and coos of her new brother.

She took her turn with the cradle board and even enjoyed the experience. She found herself secretly sharing thoughts with the small baby that she dared not voice to anyone else.

The summer hunts were good, and Running Fawn hoped most fervently that the band would return to the hills for their winter camp. Surely there would be no reason for them to stay on the prairies again. But just when she thought it was about time for them to be breaking up the summer camp, word came that there was to be another large gathering at Blackfoot Crossing along the Bow River.

The news made Running Fawn tremble. Would her world forever be in turmoil? When would things get back to normal again?

❧   ❧   ❧

September 28, 1877

Dear Brethren,

I have just witnessed a most spectacular occasion. I still have mixed feelings about the outcome, but perhaps it will work for good.

The great Blackfoot Nation gathered at Blackfoot Crossing on the Bow River to discuss the signing of a treaty. Some of the tribes to the north, the Cree, Assiniboines, and Ojibwas, signed a treaty last year. Now Chief Crowfoot has called together his people.

At first it looked like the Bloods would boycott the agreement, as only Medicine Calf, a warrior who makes no pretense about his feelings of mistrust toward the whites, was present. They needed total agreement. Finally, to the relief of the commissioners and the other chiefs, the Blood tribe arrived three days after the others had gathered. They had been greatly upset by the location for the talks. They had suggested Fort MacLeod, but Crowfoot refused to take his people to a white man's fort.

It was a spectacular site with tents stretched for miles on the prairies. I looked at it and wept. These are my people, I said to myself, feeling such love as I could never express.

They were all there—at least in representation, though many small bands were still out on the prairies in hunting parties or small camps. The Stonies wisely camped across the river, being enemies of the Black-foot. The Blackfoot and Sarcee were there in force. There were only a few Peigans present, but most of their tribe lives on the other side of the border. As soon as the Bloods arrived, Red Crow, their chief, had a meeting with Crowfoot. It was believed that he agreed to let Crowfoot, who is well known as a diplomat and orator, speak for the entire nation.

I heard the speeches, some of them stirring my heart. The Indian chiefs were eloquent, noble. Some spoke in English, some through interpreters. The representatives of the Queen seemed sincere. Yet I couldn't help but wonder how many of the promises they would actually be able to keep. I prayed silently that their word might be honored.

It was the fact of the North West Mounted Police that removed the doubts from the people. Crowfoot made a moving speech. "If the Police had not come to this country, where would we be now?" he said. "Bad men and whiskey were killing us so fast that very few of us, indeed, would have been left today. The Police have protected us as feathers of the bird protect it from the frosts of winter."

Red Crow of the proud Blood tribe also spoke. "Three years ago, when the Police first came to this country, I met and shook hands with Stamixotokon (their name for Colonel MacLeod) at Belly River. Since that time he has made me many promises. He kept them all—not one of them was ever broken. Everything that the Police have done has been good. I entirely trust Stamixotokon, and I will leave everything to him. I will sign with Crowfoot."

The other chiefs from the Blood tribe also stepped forward to sign the treaty, known as Treaty Number Seven.

The treaty gives the Indian people their own land, one square mile for every five persons, as well as other benefits. They will have hunting rights outside of the Reserve, regulated by government, and will receive an annual treaty fee of $5.00 per person, $15.00 to minor chiefs and $25.00 to head chiefs, with a bonus of $12.00 to each at the original treaty signing. They are also to get their share of $2,000.00 for a year's ammunition, a Winchester rifle, a uniform every three years for the chiefs, and flags and medals at the signing of the treaty. Believe me, the medal is important to them.

They are also to be sent teachers who will teach their children, and they will be provided with medicines to treat their illnesses as well as aid of farming tools and cattle.

At this point they seem quite pleased with the deal. There are still herds of buffalo roaming the plains, which the government officials expect to last for another ten years or so. By then they hope the Indian people will be self-sufficient in their new agricultural lifestyle. The Indians now do not feel as threatened by the white settlers who continue to move in. They know this Reserve land cannot be taken from them.

I believe that now is the time for the Christian church to seize this wonderful opportunity to provide some of the schools that will be needed. I feel excited because I believe God has directed me to the band He wishes me to serve. They are a small group from the Blackfoot tribe, nomadic as are the others, but seemingly very open. I met their chief, Calls Through The Night, at the gathering and we had many good conversations. He did not seem at all opposed to letting me join them. He even invited me into his tent to share a meal and meet his family.

He has three living children. The oldest daughter is already married to a young warrior. I didn't take to her husband—nor him to me. He seems most distrustful and sullen. However, she seemed pleasant enough. The next child, a girl, is sickly and small for her age. She has one deformed leg and walks with quite a limp. The boy, whom I would guess to be ten or eleven, is likeable and very bright. His dark eyes sparkle and he takes in everything. I have my eye on him for future leadership.

May God grant me wisdom in leading him to the way of Truth.

Living with the tribe will be enormously beneficial for my language studies.

This is a lengthy epistle, but I do covet your prayers.

Sincerely in His service,
Martin D. Forbes,
Minister of Christ.

P.S. You may be amused to know that they have favored me with an Indian name. Speaks With Full Mouth. I am hard-pressed to know if it is complimentary.

❧   ❧   ❧

Slowly the great nation began to disentangle itself and small bands scattered across the prairies. The deed was done. The treaty signed. Many were relieved that they had been instrumental in bargaining rights for their people. Many others felt misgivings. Would the future prove them to have been wrong? Others felt annoyance, even betrayal. The great chiefs should have stood and fought. The land was theirs—had always been theirs. They should have wrested it back from the white intruders—all of it. But the malcontents were few in number and hardly in the position to voice their views loudly.

Along with the little band of Calls Through The Night, a young white man sat in his saddle. He could scarcely believe his good fortune. No, not good fortune—the divine leading of Almighty God. He had been invited by the chief himself to winter with them in the distant hills. His prayer had been answered. He had been given a people. A people to love and to instruct and to lead to the Lord. His heart was full as he watched the small column move forward across the prairie. They were such beautiful, proud people. So bright of eye and strong of back.

One young man in particular had caught his attention.

The chief's son, Silver Fox, had impressed him from their first meeting over a shared meal in the chief's tent. He watched the young lad now as he called to his friend while wrestling a heavily laden travois into position behind a reluctant pony.

"Are you ready, Speaks With Full Mouth?" he called over in his native tongue when he saw Martin watching him.

"I am ready, Silver Fox," Martin replied carefully with the unfamiliar words. A delighted grin was the boy's response as he swung up on the pony.

꙳   ꙳   ꙳

Running Fawn found the measured pace of the band at odds with her inner excitement. She was going *home*. At last things had settled. They could once again be as they had been.

True, the treaty that had been signed had identified their allotted reserve as many days' travel from their usual winter campsite. But there was nothing in the treaty that required them to desert their lifestyle and stay within the confines of the Reserve. It was as her father said. There were still buffalo on the plains, still deer in the forest. There were still fish in their stream and roots and berries in the hills. There was no reason for concern. They would still be a free people.

Chapter Five

The Buffalo

Running Fawn hurried along the path, water bucket in hand. It was her first trip to the spring since returning to winter camp from the open prairies. She could hardly wait to see her favorite spot again. If she rushed, she would have some time to linger. Her mother surely would know that she needed a little while to just look and enjoy.

The stream was rather low for that time of year. For one moment Running Fawn feared it meant that the spring had stopped its flow. Without water the band could not stay.

She quickly pushed aside a willow branch that hung over the trail and peered around its sloping limb. If the spring had failed her, she would be sad indeed. But to her relief and pleasure, a first look at the rocks from which the spring was born revealed the bubbles of water gurgling forth just as she had remembered.

She breathed a deep sigh, knelt at the edge of the small basin, and reached a sun-browned hand to trail her fingers in the cold water. A few fallen leaves twirled in an eddy, and she scooped them up and lay them gently aside, then stretched her hand into the water again to enjoy its refreshing coldness. In very short order her fingers began to tingle with the chill.

"Nothing back on the plains is this cold," she whispered and took great pleasure in the knowledge that was hers.

She pushed slowly to her feet and backed up so she brushed gently against the outcropping of granite.

"I hope we never have to leave again. Never," she said quietly as she gazed off in the distance.

The bucket at her feet was forgotten as she studied the familiar sight. One large pine had fallen. Perhaps in a storm. She missed its mammoth limbs against the sky, but perhaps—just perhaps its exposed roots would make a home for the bear mother.

Thinking of the bear, she strained for a sound that would indicate its presence. Only the whisper of the wind and the gentle gurgle of the spring, with the background ripple of the small stream, reached her ears. Then a bird called. A mountain bluebird, and another answered. From the lake beyond, a loon cried. Running Fawn smiled. She was home. Home. She leaned back more firmly against the rock at her back. She would be able to spend another winter here where she belonged.

She stirred. She was not anxious to go, but her mother would be waiting for the water. Reluctantly she reached down for the pail at her feet. It was a new metal pail, recently acquired at the trading post. She would not need to haul with the clumsy bucket made of skin anymore.

"Hello," said a quiet voice, making Running Fawn jump in spite of herself. She swung around to see the strange white man sitting on a rock a few steps away. Running Fawn's first thought was of flight—but she did not have the water bucket filled.

"I'm sorry," he continued softly in her own tongue, though the words sounded different coming from his lips. "I did not mean to frighten you."

Running Fawn shrugged in careful nonchalance and turned her back to him. She would quickly dip her pail and be on her way.

"This is a . . . a beautiful place," he continued, groping for the correct words.

For a moment Running Fawn felt anger. He had no right

to her spot. Why did he think that he could intrude?

But she quickly realized how foolish the thought was. All of the small band used the path that led to the spring. All water buckets were dipped from the small basin.

"I took a walk as soon as we got into camp," he went on. "The path led me here. I'm so glad it did. It is a wonderful place for prayer."

Running Fawn straightened and looked at the strange man. He was speaking words that she did not understand.

"Prayer—" he explained gently. "Talk—with God."

She still frowned. He smiled at her and stood from his seat on the rock, but he did not approach her.

"Did you ever wonder how this all came to be? Who created this . . . this beauty? It was God. God the Creator of all things. This Book—" He held up the hand that was holding a strange-looking black book. "This is the Book that tells about Him. It is called the Bible. When I talk to Him—it is called prayer."

He waited. Running Fawn did not respond, but she couldn't help but be drawn to his words. How could that object—the Book—tell about God?

"That is why I have come here—to live with your people. I want to tell you all about this Book. About the God of all"—he flung one long arm in a big arc—"this."

Running Fawn did not know whether to listen further or to dash for the safety of the camp.

"Your mother will be waiting for the water," he said gently. "We can talk more later."

Quickly Running Fawn knelt to swish aside small intruders on the pond surface and scoop her bucket full of water.

Without even a backward glance she ran down the path that led back to the village. The whole encounter had unsettled her—but she wasn't sure just why. At least she now knew why the man had come to stay with them. He came to talk about the Black Book. Running Fawn had never seen a book before. She had no idea what it was all about, but she felt a strange stirring of curiosity. She wished she were brave enough to take the Book in her own hands.

In spite of their white visitor, they all quickly settled back into camp life. The young man was seen talking with this warrior or that, and often with the chief. On several occasions, Running Fawn even saw him chat with the young boys. She wondered if he was showing them the Black Book. She longed to take a peek at it herself but stayed at a distance, quickly dipping into the bush or dashing behind a tent if she saw the white man coming her way.

She now dreaded the trips to the stream and always made sure she went in the company of other young girls. She felt cheated. Like she had given up a part of her own self.

And then one night the chief announced that there would be a meeting around the open fire. The white man had something he wished to say and they all would be there to listen. Running Fawn felt both curiosity and panic. What could the white man say that would be of interest to her people—to her?

When the last chores of the day had been completed, the open fire was built in the middle of the camp. Running Fawn followed closely behind her mother, who led little Bright Star by the hand. The baby had now outgrown the cradle board and wished to toddle along with the family, but he still needed a hand, as his little feet were prone to trip over small roots or uneven ground. Moon Over Trees smiled good-naturedly and patiently helped her little son to his feet again.

They settled close to the circle, blanket shawls wrapped around their shoulders to keep away the chill of the mountain night.

When the chief was assured that all were present, he stood to his feet. He was a commanding presence in spite of the ravages of time and a nomadic life.

"We have come," he began, "to listen to our white friend

who has something important to tell us. I have listened for many nights. I have heard his words and they speak to my heart. Now I wish you to hear his words. What he says is a new sound. He calls it Truth. He speaks of a god we do not know. A god who he says made all things. The rivers, the mountains, the trees, the buffalo. What he says is strange. If it is a right way, I do not know. Listen. We will listen together and then we will decide if it is right." He sat down and folded his blanket closely about his shriveled frame.

The white man now stood. In the light of the fire and the glow of the rising moon, his face looked pale and glistening. If she had met him along a wooded trail, Running Fawn was sure she would have run away in fright.

He lifted the Black Book that he always seemed to have in his hand and began to talk to the people. His voice was quiet but powerful as he slowly and carefully chose his words.

"Long, long ago, before the sun was in the day sky or the moon lighted the night, before man walked on earth or the deer fed in the forest, there was God. A great God. He had always been. Had never been born to the tepee. Had never grown in the cradle board. He had never had mother or father—for He is God. Without Him, nothing would be—for He is the maker of all things. He planted the forests and placed the mountains and the valleys. He started the streams and rivers flowing and formed the lakes at the foot of the hills. He put the buffalo on the plains and the bear in the woodlands. He showed the geese how to fly and the loon how to swim.

"Then He said, 'I will make man—in my likeness'—and He did. Man, and woman, his helpmate, were the greatest of His creation. Mankind was made good. God loved His creation.

"But mankind did not stay good. They did wrong. They went against the command of God. They spoiled the good world He had made. God said, 'Because you have disobeyed my word, you will die.'

"For many years the world got worse and worse, but God still loved His people. He still longed to have them obey Him. So He had a plan. He gave them laws to follow—laws that would honor Him. Instead of facing death for their wrongs, He let them offer an animal to die in their place. But they could not keep the laws. They kept making bad choices and doing wrong. Their hearts were selfish—wishing to have their brothers' land and horses, cheating and killing one another. But God had another part to His plan. This part showed God's great love. Doing wrong still meant death. But God loved His people. He did not wish for them to die. So He sent His Son—His only Son. 'My Son will die in their place,' said God. 'He will pay the penalty of death for them.'

"And He did. His Son Jesus died for wicked mankind. He paid the death penalty. He wants to give His people new hearts—to love Him and to love each other. We must be sorry for our evil hearts and ask Him for a new one. This Book— the Bible—tells us how we are to live. I have come here to tell you of its message. It has been given for all people. The white, the Blackfoot, the Cree, the Stoney, the Sarcee. All people. All people were made by the one true God. All people have done wrong. But Jesus, the Son of the only true God, has died for all people of the earth. God wants them to be brothers."

Running Fawn was sure that the white man had more words to speak, but the chief now stood shakily to his feet. The young man lowered his upraised hand that held the Black Book. Courteously he stepped back into the shadows.

"We will hear more on another night," announced the chief, his tone giving hint of what he thought about these strange new ideas.

Running Fawn was disappointed. The story had been interesting. She had never heard a tale around the fire that had so gripped her attention. She wished they could hear it all. She wanted to know more about this great God of whom the young white man spoke.

But Chief Calls Through The Night was already wrap-

56

ping his blankets closely around his frail shoulders and moving off toward his own tent where the fire would take the chill from his elderly bones.

❧   ❧   ❧

Night after night they gathered around the campfire and heard more stories from the Black Book. Still the chief was held back, not pushing his people for a decision. Some were ready to accept the words. Others had grave doubts. "That is the white man's god," they argued. "We have Mother Earth and the Sun God. They have always cared for our people."

Running Fawn was torn between a desire to accept the words as truth and a fear that they might be wrong. What if she accepted them and the Sun God became angry? She shivered at the very thought.

❧   ❧   ❧

For days a cloud of acrid smoke hung over the sheltered valley. The villagers did not need to be told the meaning. Somewhere there was a fire.

Scouts were sent out. Each time they returned with the same report. There seemed to be no fire near enough to them to threaten the camp.

But the dark, murky cloud persisted in drifting into the camp on every wind that blew their way.

At last one brave brought back a different story. It was the plain. The whole plain had been swept by fierce monster fires. Tribes had needed to flee to the north or to the mountains. Panicked into trying to outrun the flame, the buffalo had stampeded south. It was the most widespread destruction of the prairies by fire that any of the chiefs could remember. There would be no food, no game on the burned-out grasslands. Only the fish in the streams had survived the fiery onslaught. It would be a long, bleak winter until the coming again of spring. It struck fear in every heart.

"They will return. Come spring, the buffalo will return," comforted Chief Calls Through The Night.

The words of their wise chief were enough to put their minds at ease.

ψ   ψ   ψ

Spring did come again, and preparation was made to leave the winter campground and go in the search of buffalo. Dried pemmican and fresh venison or rabbit had gotten them through the long winter, but now the camp was in need of buffalo. Buffalo roasts for cooking pots, buffalo meat for the pemmican strips, buffalo skins for robes and new tent skins, buffalo bones for utensils. So they once again set off on the trail of the mighty beast.

When they reached the plains after many days of hard travel, they were met by other nomadic bands. Always the word was the same. There were no buffalo in sight. All of the mighty beasts had vacated the plains before the fire. All had crossed the border into Montana. They were now being hunted by the brothers in the south.

Through the long, hot days of summer, the small band hunted for game. There was never enough to fill the empty bellies. Women and children grew weaker and weaker. Many died, among them the chief's sickly daughter. It was enough. The chief announced that they would follow the Blood Nation into Montana Territory where the great beasts could still be found.

It was a long, arduous journey. Running Fawn had not known that the world was so big. It stretched mile after mile, and always when one climbed a hill there was another hill beyond. She was sure they would never make it. Her mother became ill and could no longer walk. Running Fawn and her sister Little Brook had to shoulder extra bundles as room was cleared on the travois to make a place for their sick mother and little brother. The heavier loads soon had shoulders drooping with fatigue, but no complaint was voiced.

Running Fawn even managed a smile and a cheerful comment for Bright Star on occasion, as he waved to her from his perch beside their mother.

Day after day they tramped on. Surely they would all be dead before they could reach their destination.

The white man stayed with them. Daily he went out with the hunting parties. His original wearing apparel had become so tattered that he had long since thrown them away and dressed in buckskins—but even they were showing the wear of the trail. He was weak from malnutrition and browned from the burning sun, but still he refused to leave the staggering band and take refuge in one of the small settlements of other white people along the trail.

Around the campfire at night, he still pulled out his Black Book and shared stories of great men and women who had lived in the first beginnings. The stories were a diversion to tired bodies and weary minds. But the people seemed to see them as only that. Stories. Amusing tales to distract them from their grim circumstance. Running Fawn wasn't sure, but she thought they were more than mere stories to him.

But eventually even the white man's eyes reflected the same despair as in the faces of her people. Would they be able to endure? Would they all be lost? Did his fervent prayers really do any good?

Then one day, they struggled slowly up one more hill— and there they were. A small but very welcome herd of rangy buffalo, feeding on the brown prairie grass or lying contently and chewing their cud in the heat of the afternoon sun.

A cheer would have gone up—but throats were parched and muscles were aching and no one wanted to even whisper, lest the herd vanish like a mirage before their very eyes. Silently they withdrew to the shadows of the hills and wearily set up another camp.

❧   ❧   ❧

The kill the next day brought great relief and rejoicing.

Running Fawn was among the women who followed the hunters. They sang as they skinned the shaggy beasts, their sharp knives making quick work of the task before them. She was not yet strong enough for the initial skinning, but she helped cut up the meat.

That evening the smoke from the campfires was seasoned with the warm, rich odor of roasting flesh. Fresh skins hung over poles or lay in heaped bundles. People called good-naturedly to one another. Heavy shoulders lifted and aching muscles were forgotten.

Where there were buffalo, there was plenty. Soon too-lean bodies would be fleshed out again and strength would return to weakened arms and legs. Tent skins could be replaced, so that the harsh prairie wind could be kept beyond the entrance flap. Bone needles and coarse thread could be made for stitching tents and clothing and moccasins. Yes, the buffalo meant life and health and a future to Running Fawn's people.

Chapter Six

Loss

The Reverend Martin Forbes stretched comfortably before his own worn tent. His back ached, his arms felt weighted, but he smiled softly to himself as he remembered the feast and enjoyed the feeling of a satisfied stomach. God had answered prayer. The people had been saved from sure disaster. There was food for the body.

He bowed his head in deep gratitude to God who had provided—then added to his prayer a further petition.

"Lord, may they soon be as interested in food for their souls."

᙭ ᙭ ᙭

During the summer that followed, they were forced to break camp often in order to follow the small herds, but they did not mind the travel. As long as they had buffalo, their world was secure. And so they stayed south of the border, even through the winter, the next spring, and another summer.

But many other small Indian bands had made the same arduous trek. And each one knew that beyond the hills were other hunters. The Peigans, the Bloods, and Sarcee from beyond the border had crossed to hunt, joining the tribes that already counted the Montana plains as their hunting grounds. Running Fawn heard the elders' concerns that the buffalo were being depleted too quickly.

There were a few minor skirmishes as hunters contested the hunting rights, but no major confrontations took place. Each band knew that the herds were vanishing. That the few buffalo that remained would not last for long. It brought both anxiety and a strange generosity. Underlying the tensions of past wars and hatred for enemy tribes was a common bond of unity. They were of one skin. They were brothers. They must all live—or die—together.

So they eyed with mutual suspicion and distaste the wood-frame settlements and the scattered white dwellers who plowed under the prairie grasses and fenced the land with sharp barbed wire.

It was no wonder that the settlers' steers disappeared from rangelands, even though beef, having less flavor than the wild meat, was not the Indians' preference.

It was *their* land. Had always been their land. Theirs to hunt. Theirs to dispute. Theirs to fight over until the strong forced out the weak. It had always been so.

But now they were helpless to show their strength. Enemy guns, carried by blue-coated soldiers, outnumbered their own weapons. Striking out at the conquering would only bring deadly reprisal.

And so they moved in a daze through the heated months of summer, following the diminishing herds, pretending in their hearts that the buffalo would always be there, that the *mother* herd was just over the next rise of hills.

But it was not to be. By the time the autumn breezes were bending low the browned prairie grasses, the last of the buffalo had been slaughtered. The great herds were no more.

Around the campfires, impassioned discussions concluded that surely there were still buffalo to be hunted. They might be just beyond the camp, just beyond that row of hills. But hunting scouts returned from far afield bringing the disturbing news that no buffalo were to be seen.

Perhaps the animals had gone back north across the border. But eventually word came that no animals were seen across the vast Canadian plains either.

A few wise elders came to the conclusion that the Sun God, angry that the tribes had let in the white settlers to desecrate the land, had made a huge hole in the ground and had run the large herds into the bowels of the earth. Their source of food and clothing and livelihood had been totally consumed. The people were stunned. Lost. Bewildered. Had their gods forsaken them? The nightly ceremonies and dancing seemed to go unanswered. They were a people set adrift in an unknown, uncaring world.

❧ ❧ ❧

There was nothing to do but to return home to familiar territory. Chief Calls Through The Night gave his order to break camp one crisp spring morning when the wind from the north still carried a hint of late skiffs of snow.

It was not a wise time to be making such a long trek over open prairie, but there was no choice. Montana would not sustain them longer.

Wearily they dismantled their tents and packed their bundles for the long journey. But exactly where it might take them—and how many of their number would actually arrive at the destination—were questions no one asked aloud.

Running Fawn secretly feared for her mother. She had not really gained back her strength since the long trip south when she had become ill. Would the return trip be too much for her?

Moon Over Trees insisted on walking as the trek began. Running Fawn fell in step beside her, anxious but afraid to speak. By the end of the first day's journey, she noticed that her mother's usual firm step was already faltering. Day by day the wind became more bitter, the rations more scarce. Soon members of the small band were coughing, others were gasping for sufficient air, and the pace of the whole group slowed considerably.

By the end of the sixth day they buried the first body. From then on it seemed to be a somber part of each day's march. As the numbers slowly dwindled, old folk, children, the weak, and the worn gradually disappeared from the evening campfires.

Running Fawn's fear clamped her stomach in knots. Her mother had taken to riding the travois now. She barely had the strength to build the cooking fire at the end of the day. Fortunately, Bright Star seemed not to be suffering from the journey. For that Running Fawn was thankful. The small child would keep her mother fighting to live.

❧   ❧   ❧

By the time they reached their old winter's campsite in the sheltering arms of the Rockies, the band was half the size it had been when they had left it. Running Fawn, beginning her eleventh winter, was so glad to be back again. Surely now in these familiar, beloved surroundings things would return to normal. Surely now her mother, who was still clinging to life, would get completely well. There were no buffalo in their hills, but they could make do with the deer and elk and moose. The animals had always provided for their needs in the past, and they would continue to sustain the band now. There was no need to trek out to the plains each summer. There were no more buffalo to hunt. They could live in their hills—forever.

❧   ❧   ❧

Life returned to its rhythm and routine. Running Fawn picked up her bucket and headed down the familiar path to the spring. Her first action upon arrival was to carefully scan the entire area to make sure that she was alone. Assured that the white missionary was not occupying a seat on a nearby rock, she lowered her pail to the ground and stepped back until her shoulder gently brushed the granite rock.

They were later than usual in setting up the winter camp, and snow already dusted the landscape with white. That long trail home from Montana had seemed to stretch farther with every step they took, but now they were home. Back where they belonged.

Running Fawn sighed in contentment. There was a security in the wind brushing through the pine needles. A security in the soft murmur of the nearby stream, still not entirely frozen over. And there was security in the cold, solid rock at her back. It had always been there—and forever would be. Surely that made one breathe a little easier. Just knowing that some things did not change.

ᵛᵏ   ᵛᵏ   ᵛᵏ

It had been a difficult time for the people, the young missionary wrote from the blankets where he lay. He had not been well, had in fact been sure at one point that he would not live to complete the arduous return to the hill country, but God had spared him. He paused, pen in hand, as he lay propped up on his bed of buffalo robes. He felt that he must get some kind of report back to the Mission Society—but what could he say? How could he possibly make them understand his situation—the situation of his people?

So he wrote simply, "It has been a difficult time for the people."

There was no use trying to describe the frustration, the pain, the death. There were no words to make them feel a part of, or understand, the suffering. Better to just leave the details unspecified.

The buffalo herds had been depleted, he went on to explain.

This will mean hardship for the entire Blackfoot Nation. Some small bands have straggled onto the Reserve set aside for them, but they are proud, strong people. Most of them wish to make their own way. Chief

Calls Through The Night is one of those. He is determined to keep his people *free* for as long as he is able.

They have already suffered the loss of half of the
small band. Others are weak, and should any type of
sickness strike the camp, many more will die.

I have as yet to make a convert. Chief Calls
Through The Night has seemed interested in the Gospel and has so many times seemed close to accepting.
But he holds back. Most of the band would not make a
step of faith until the chief does. It is their way. Some
seem to be ready, but they refuse to break from old
ways.

I trust now that we are back in our own camp that
I will be able to start classes with the children. I pray
that this might be the answer to our prayers.

> Yours in Him, whom I serve,
> Martin D. Forbes,
> Minister of the Gospel.

P.S. The band has given me a new name, and one that
I prefer. I am now known in the Blackfoot tongue as
Man With The Book.

⚜   ⚜   ⚜

Running Fawn was surprised when the chief announced
that Man With The Book would begin classes, and she was
chosen as one of the children to attend. The school would be
held in a special tent erected for that very purpose. Though
she secretly admitted that she did have some curiosity, she
was not flattered by the invitation. In the days preceding the
actual start of the school, she busied herself with tasks close
by her mother's fire. There was an uncertainty—a gnawing
fear about learning from the white man.

The chief seemed pleased with the arrangement. "Our
world changes," he had told the gathering. "We must change.
The White man is here to stay. We must learn his ways." He
nodded toward the young missionary, still weak and thin
from his illness, but smiling softly nonetheless. "Man With

The Book teach. He teach the son of my old age," the chief concluded, drawing his robes tightly around frail shoulders and nodding toward Silver Fox, who sat quietly, legs crossed.

There were a total of six children selected for the school. Running Fawn knew them all, though she and the other girl in the group had spent little time with the four boys. Laughing Loon was a bit older than Running Fawn and was much more outgoing. In Running Fawn's mind, the young Silver Fox was almost a man. She wondered why the young brave should waste his time with lessons and books. The other three boys were younger than he was.

In spite of her reluctance to learn from the white man, Running Fawn soon found herself caught up in the classes. Her inquisitive mind reached eagerly for new knowledge. But it was Silver Fox who proved to be the natural student. Running Fawn noticed that the missionary teacher spent extra time with the young brave.

Before too many weeks had passed, one of the boys dropped out. He simply had no interest in learning and thus disrupted the rest of the class. Man With The Book did all he could to peak the lad's interest, but nothing seemed to engage him. At last the missionary conceded defeat, at least for the present, and allowed the boy to withdraw.

All through the long months of winter, the small class met to study in their makeshift classroom. Cold days just drew them in closer to the fire, making eyes sting with woodsmoke as they strained to read the unfamiliar letters on their teacher's chalkboard, then reproduce them with pieces of charcoal on slabs of wood.

"I will get paper and pencils for you as soon as I can," he promised, showing them the precious items from his limited stores.

But Running Fawn found it hard to let herself go, to become fully involved in the joy of learning. In taking in this new world, she feared that she was losing her grip on the old. Something about seeing Silver Fox throw himself wholeheartedly into the excitement of the strange English words and of the printed page brought fear to her heart. On the one hand, she could not but admire his keen mind. But on the other, she felt that he was, in some way she could not explain, betraying his people. To further confuse matters, she was beginning to be aware that Silver Fox was a ruggedly attractive young man and one at whom other girls her age cast silent, inviting glances.

And he was kind and thoughtful, often helping the younger students to learn a new lesson, carefully explaining it in their own tongue, then translating the words to the difficult English ones. Running Fawn always flushed, disturbed and confused, when he bent close to help her. She could not understand her own reaction.

How could she admire yet distrust him at the same time? While she felt drawn to him, something deep within her sent her warning signals. He seemed too at home with learning, with the white man's world. On the other hand, her mind argued, he was the chief's son. Surely he would not turn his back on his own people. His father wished him to learn the white man's language and ways. He was simply acting in obedience. But he seemed to enjoy the lessons so. Was it wise? And was it wise to be reading in the white man's Black Book? Every free moment he had he seemed to be turning the thin pages.

Running Fawn was confused. Her mind kept working at the problem, but she could not arrive at a satisfactory answer.

"Fire!"

The cry rang out in the darkness of the winter's night. Running Fawn startled awake, felt her blood run cold. It was the most dreaded word in the camp. Fire could sweep over all the tent homes in a matter of minutes. Whose tent? Whose tent was burning?

Even before she could disentangle herself from the robes,

her father, followed closely by her mother, was out of the tent. Excited voices called to one another, "Fire. Fire."

Running Fawn crawled to the opening of the tent and snatched the flap back with trembling hand. At first she saw nothing except for milling bodies, but she could smell intense smoke in the air. She pushed herself through the opening and stood on shaking legs. The smoke was dense now. She could smell it and taste it and it made her eyes sting. Then she heard a shout.

"It's the school tent!"

The school tent was set apart from the others—to avoid distractions, Man With The Book had said. It stood near the edge of the stream, not even under the shelter of the large pine boughs nearby.

Running Fawn let out her breath. Perhaps . . . perhaps if they were fortunate—if the gods were not too angry, they could save the rest of the camp.

She hurried along with the crowd that made its way toward the stream. Already dark figures silhouetted against the flames were fighting the blaze. Someone was swinging an axe to chop a hole in the ice for water. Another was beating at the fire with a length of buffalo skin. Others crowded close and threw handfuls of snow into the flames. Another man was hurriedly chopping down a pine that might be too close to the flaming structure and could spread the fire to the rest of the village.

In a short time it was all over. The school tent had not been saved—but all the rest of the village had been spared. After some discussion of how the fire had started—no doubt a stray spark from a campfire—weary, smoke-blackened bodies returned to their beds to attempt further sleep.

Running Fawn was fighting her own continuing silent battle. She felt sorry for Man With The Book who had fought valiantly until the last spark was extinguished, yet she could not but feel a sense of relief. There would be no more school. No more tempting of the Sun God. She could relax now. The old way was secured. They would not learn any more ways and words of the white man.

She was turning away from the scene when she spotted a solitary figure who still stood silently in the light of the moon. Silver Fox, head bowed, shoulders slumped, stared fixedly at the smoldering heap that symbolized his hope for learning. Running Fawn had never seen such disappointment on a face. Perhaps . . . perhaps she had been selfish in her personal desires.

Chapter Seven

To the Plains

The spring sun reached down fingers of warmth, melting
the banks of snow and freeing the frozen stream to sing
again. Returning geese honked joyously overhead, and the
loon called from the lake waters released from winter's icy
prison. It was Running Fawn's favorite time of the year. She
found it hard not to skip in her eagerness as she picked up
the water bucket and headed down the path that led to the
spring.

On the way she saw small boys noisily trying to outdo one
another as they skipped stones in the creek waters. She
merely smiled and passed on by. Life was good. They had
made it through another chilling winter. Had returned once
again to the warmth of the sun. There had been wild meat
for the cooking pots and wood for the fires. Her mother had
gradually gained strength. No serious illnesses had visited
the camp. All was right with the world.

Her eyes quickly scanned the spring site to see if others
might be there ahead of her. When she was assured that she
was alone, she let her pail slide from her fingers and pushed
herself up against the rock. There was a coldness to the granite, for the tall pines shaded it from the sun's new warmth.
But she liked the feel of it, cool and strong against her shoulder. She pushed a little closer to it and let her eyes wander
out over the valley before her. In the sky a lone hawk circled,

crying in the stillness of the morning air as he made his graceful arcs on silent currents.

Near at hand she heard the chattering squirrels as they quarreled over a food supply. Then a rabbit, half brown fur, half white, darted from among a tangled web of upturned tree roots and hurried off down the path, uplifted tail forever white making a waving flag behind him.

It was difficult to pull away from her reverie, but at length she sighed, dipped the pail in the shallow pool of new spring water, and headed back toward the camp.

Spring, she mused inwardly. *Other years we would be preparing to break camp. This year? This year we will be able to stay throughout the entire summer. There will be no striking down of tents, no bundling heavy burdens. No need to move out. The buffalo are gone. Gone.*

And although the thought was troubling because of what it meant to the tribes, it also brought a measure of consolation. If the buffalo herds still roamed the plains, they would follow them. Now she would be able to enjoy her favorite spot all year round.

❧   ❧   ❧

June 3, 1881

Dear Brethren,

We are still at the winter camp, but I do not know how long we shall remain here. I have not tried to resume classes since the burning of our tent school that I previously reported on to you. It did not seem feasible to do so with my scant supply of teaching materials lost to the flames. However, Silver Fox, the chief's son, still studies with me. He has great promise.

I have enjoyed long talks with Chief Calls Through The Night. He tells me he wishes to learn more from the Black Book, as he calls the Bible. But he has reservation about accepting the words of the Book.

It is not that he wouldn't like to accept them. It is

that he is afraid to give up the Indian teachings that have been handed down to him from his father and grandfather. If I could truthfully say that he could embrace the two faiths as one, I am sure he would have no hesitation. But I cannot do that. The Bible is clear that there is only one God and only one path that leads to Him.

I have such a love for these beautiful people. My heart yearns to bring them to Christ. I pray daily for wisdom in teaching them to know and accept the truth. Surely God, in His majesty and mercy, would be proud to call them His own.

The chief knows that the buffalo are gone. He still clings to the hope that the people will be able to survive on other game. It will be difficult with so many hunters seeking sustenance, but he insists that Mother Earth will not let them perish. I wish I could help him to understand that only God can supply the needs of the people.

I think that Silver Fox does understand. At least in part. But he is reluctant to disgrace his father by taking on a new religion. There is a great depth to the boy and a remarkable understanding of their situation. He will make a great statesman for his people.

❧   ❧   ❧

"We break camp at first light."

Chief Calls Through The Night stood, enshrouded in his blanket wrap, his hand lifted to his people as he made the announcement.

Running Fawn was stunned. How could it be? Where would they go? What was the reason for leaving their mountain home?

Question after question raced through her mind, but she had no opportunity to ask them.

The chief had already dismissed the assembly, turning

and slowly making his way back over the footpath to his tepee.

There was silence. Total silence. People did not even stir.
They looked at one another blankly, faces robbed of all expression. Then silently, heads down, they began to move toward their tents, steps silent on moccasined feet.

But why? Running Fawn anguished over the question.
Why? What can we gain by moving camp?

She did not cry out. Did not even whisper. Her father answered some of her questions as he explained in a soft voice
to her mother, "Chief fears for the people. Most game gone
back into hills. Our last hunts were bad. No game. We will
need food soon now."

Her mother did not question either man but nodded her
head solemnly.

They will come back. They will come back! Running Fawn
wished to argue, but she knew that she was being foolish.
The deer and elk would not return until after they had borne
their young and cared for them on the high meadow grasses.
The chief was right. They had to break camp.

⚜   ⚜   ⚜

For two long months the little band ranged over the prairies, finding scant food supplies and becoming more hungry
and more discouraged. Again weakened bodies threatened to
succumb to illness or starvation. At last the chief could hold
out no longer. After many consultations with the elders, he
called the group together and issued his decision.

"We will go," he said sadly, his silver head bowed in sub-
mission, his once proud shoulders drooping in resignation.
"We will go to Reserve land. We will take the treaty money.
We can get food. We will go at first light."

Although there was sorrow at this step away from freedom and dignity, there was also unexpressed relief. At least
there would be food. At least there would be shelter. They
also would be among their own people, for many bands of the

great Blackfoot Nation had already gathered on the Reserve. It really could not be too bad. Could it?

Running Fawn's small community adjusted more quickly to life on the Reserve than expected. Already some Blackfoot who had been there for the last two years had planted gardens and were raising crops in broken prairie sod. A few log homes were scattered among the many tepees that dotted the plains, and the owners moved in and out, back and forth, between the two kinds of dwellings as suited their fancy. Running Fawn could not imagine herself in a wooden home. How could one breathe freely? How would the smoke from the fire escape through the solid roof? It did not seem like a healthy or a comfortable way to live.

The little group had arranged for their own piece of land and set up their tepees. Nearby dogs barked and children pointed as the new occupants set about making these prairie lands their home.

Running Fawn let her eyes drift over the area around them. Where was the stream? The spring for a water supply? She knew the Bow River lay just over the nearby hills, but surely one did not need to make daily treks all the way to its banks through the heat of the summer sun to fill the water buckets? Eventually she saw a strange-looking apparatus with a wooden handle that someone was working vigorously up and down until a small stream of water poured from its iron mouth. Here was where one filled the buckets, she was told. But it was still a long way from their tepee settlement. It was almost closer to walk to the river.

But they were not given a choice. Those responsible for the welfare of the Indian people explained that all water for cooking or drinking must be taken from the hole in the ground—the well—for the sake of their health.

It puzzled Running Fawn. They had been drinking from the streams and rivers all their lives.

She would close her ears to the words and follow the ways of her people.

❧   ❧   ❧

As the weeks slipped by, Running Fawn felt the tension and inner turmoil slowly slipping away—for though much had changed, much was still the same.

They lived, to a large part, as they had always lived. There were the hunting parties who left the camp each morning and, more often than not, returned with game by day's end. There were still the sturdy tepees lifting their proud heads toward the blue of the sky. There were still the busy women, bent over tanning skin or stirring the cooking pot. There were still the campfires, lazily sending curls of blue-gray smoke into the haze of twilight, even though now it came from hundreds of campfires scattered throughout the hilly plains.

The slender girl, now grown strong and skillful in Indian ways, even promised herself that come the next spring, she would learn how to plant a garden and make the turnips, potatoes, onions, and carrots readily available for the cooking pots.

And then her world changed again. She was informed by the smiling Man With The Book that the chief had authorized a new tent school, and she was one of the fortunate ones who would be returning to classes.

Her heart sank. She had no desire for more lessons. More learning, yes. Lessons from the white man's books, no. But when she glanced toward her father, she read in his eyes such pride that she knew he would not understand the disappointment of her heart. She lowered her eyes in submission. When the classes began again, she knew she would be in attendance.

❧   ❧   ❧

In spite of her reluctance, she worked hard at school. She had a natural thirst for learning, and she told herself that if she learned quickly all that was intended for her, she would soon be done and be able to go about her normal life again.

In spite of her diligence, she could not keep up to Silver Fox, who was still eagerly studying in spite of his years.

All through the winter months and into the spring they pored over their books. Running Fawn was greatly relieved when the missionary announced that they would take a break for the planting season. She stood in line at the small post for her allotment of garden seed and learned from a neighbor how to place them in the warm prairie soil. Soon little sprouts were raising their heads to reach for sun, and Running Fawn's heart quickened. She tended them as she would have cared for a child. Watering them when they appeared thirsty. Plucking weeds from her patch as soon as they dared show a leaf. Gently hoeing and hilling, and quickly dispatching any intruding insects.

But Silver Fox kept right on studying. No longer joining the hunting parties, he seemed totally absorbed in learning. Driven to discovering something new in the books. Hungry for knowledge. Running Fawn could not understand his passion.

In the fall, classes began again. A number of younger children joined them, now in a small wooden building. Running Fawn gladly would have given up her seat to any one of them.

❧   ❧   ❧

"Who are they?" Running Fawn asked her friend Laughing Loon as they peered at two unfamiliar white men in long-tailed black coats who were approaching their settlement.

"I not know," whispered Laughing Loon, even though the distance between them and the men would have made it impossible to hear a normal voice.

They were used to strangers visiting the Reserve. They

came in fancy eastern dress representing the Queen on government business. They came representing the law, dressed in scarlet tunics and astride leather saddles. They came as traders in the garb of frontiersmen, seeking beaded leather goods in exchange for pots or bullets. But these two men looked like none of the others. Running Fawn frowned.

The two friends watched as the strangers were greeted by the chief and admitted with ceremony into his tent. Then the girls were distracted by a group of boys who wrestled on the stiff brown grasses, trying to prove to one another—or to the girls—which was the strongest. Mostly they proved which was the loudest.

It was not until the next morning that Running Fawn had cause to remember the two visitors. When she entered the school building, they stood before the class, broad smiles lighting pale faces, hands tucked neatly behind their tailed coats. Silently Running Fawn slipped onto the bench behind the wooden desk, her eyes traveling quickly to Man With The Book.

He smiled around at the class and then at her, seeming very pleased with himself—or something.

"Class," he began as soon as they had repeated the Lord's Prayer and sang the verse of a hymn, "we have good news. Two of our students have been chosen to attend advanced classes at the Mission Boarding School in Fort Calgary."

He paused expectantly and looked again around the room. But it was with stunned bewilderment that Running Fawn heard the words.

The man with the biggest grin and blackest coat stepped forward. "We have already spoken with Chief Calls Through The Night. He is proud to send his best students for further learning."

Running Fawn could not refrain from casting a sideways glance at Silver Fox. Everyone in the school knew who the best pupil was. But even he looked surprised.

The man now stepped back, his grin just as wide, his coattails flapping slightly in the breeze that came in the opened window.

"I will let your teacher make the announcement," he said, as though bestowing a singular honor.

Man With The Book cleared his throat and flushed slightly. Then he took a step closer to his class.

"First I wish to inform you that if you study hard, this great opportunity may one day be yours as well. . . . Now— let me congratulate our first students to be allowed to study at the Mission School. You are indeed a credit to your families and to your chief."

He stopped again and his small mustache twitched slightly.

"Silver Fox, may I congratulate you." He held out his hand.

For one moment Silver Fox looked stunned. Then a small, quiet smile began to lift the corners of his lips as he stood to his feet and accepted the outstretched hand.

He was pleased. Running Fawn had known he would be.

"And the second student," continued the teacher after he had completed the hearty handshake and turned slightly to face the other side of the room, "Running Fawn."

It was like a loud clap of thunder. Like the sickening roar of an avalanche. Like lightning smashing into a towering pine. Running Fawn felt the world whirling around, making her dizzy with flashing light and deafening sound. She could not move. Could not speak. Could not even swallow.

She was dimly aware that there was movement before her. That someone stood before her desk, hand outstretched, but she could not respond. Could not even think.

"I do believe our student is dumbstruck," said a teasing voice that seemed to roar in her ears. A giggle was heard somewhere near her and began to spread throughout the room. Gradually she felt herself returning to reality.

She managed to stumble from her desk and stretch out a limp hand to be clasped firmly by the teacher. Then she was allowed to sink back onto the support of the wooden bench as she fought to gather her wits about her and make some sense of the announcement.

The boarding school. In Fort Calgary. She did not want to go to the boarding school. Let Silver Fox learn the ways of the white man if he wished to. She wanted no part of it. None whatever. No. No, she had no intention of going. She would speak to her father. He knew that she was needed at home. Her mother still was not strong. And another child was on the way. Her mother needed her. She wouldn't go. She would not.

She tried to clear her head. She looked up just in time to see the pair of long-tailed coats disappearing out the door. She hoped she had seen the last of them.

She felt eyes upon her and turned slightly to discover Silver Fox looking at her. He gave her the slightest smile just before she dipped her head in confusion.

❧   ❧   ❧

The next morning, the two men with the black suits sat in a black buggy hitched to a pair of gray horses. Silver Fox occupied the high seat behind them, his eyes shining, his back straight. Running Fawn slowly mounted the steps into the buggy, her movements stiff and her heart heavy with fear and frustration.

She sat as close to the far edge of the seat as she could, gripping firmly the small bundle that was all she would have of home. She longed to weep. Longed to cling desperately to her mother's skirts. Longed to streak across the broad prairies until she found a hiding place.

She did nothing. Just sat, tight-lipped and stiff. Shivering inside, and silent and cold on the outside. Someone called to her, but she did not so much as turn her head. Stoically she stared straight in front of her at the broad back of the man in the black coat.

He lifted the buggy whip, spoke to the horses, and they began to move out of the camp. The big wheels turned round and round. The buggy bumped over prairie-dog holes. Dust began to lift in little clouds until she felt she would choke. But she did not turn her head. Did not look back. She would not look back all the long way to the unknown Calgary.

Chapter Eight

Boarding School

On the first night they stopped at the home of white settlers, and she was shown to a small lean-to room at the back of the house. A strange-looking frame on one side of the room held blankets, and Running Fawn looked at them with longing. She was extremely weary and ached for her buffalo robe bed. But there was no such place in sight. After the door had closed, Running Fawn furtively looked about, then reached to snatch the top blanket from the pile. Wrapping it securely about her, she lay down on the crude wooden floor and wept silently until she fell into a troubled sleep.

The next morning after a rather strange breakfast, they were on the way again. That night they stopped at another small farmhouse. Running Fawn was given a blanket and, with many apologies, shown to a loft over the kitchen. The small storage area had been stacked with soft hay. It was much more comfortable than the bare boards of the night before.

They rumbled on over the rutted prairie for the next day, stopping at a small settlement, where they were all taken into a large building with many rooms. Again there was a frame with blankets, and again Running Fawn took the top one and curled up on the floor. This floor was covered with a strange kind of blanket all its own. Running Fawn found it much softer than the bare planks.

From then on she stopped counting. Stopped thinking.
Day after day they traveled, and night after night they
stopped in one strange place after the other.

Running Fawn had spoken no word since leaving the Reserve. Silver Fox passed questions from the two black-coated
men on to her and she nodded or shook her head, her only
response. She did not want to speak to the white men, even
though she recognized most of the words they used. She did
not like the white men, nor their self-proclaimed mission
that was taking her far from her home and family. She had
no intention of responding to any of their rather obvious
overtures of friendship.

They allowed for frequent stops and moments of privacy.
For that, Running Fawn was grudgingly grateful.

They ate more strange food along the way. Roasted beef
wrapped between pieces of bread. Bits of dried fruits that
were bigger than any berries Running Fawn had ever seen,
and different flavors as well. These white people mixed various things in big pots and let them simmer and simmer.
Running Fawn had never tasted these dishes before and did
not like the taste now. They drank hot drinks, cooked over
an open fire, even though the days were warm and a cool
drink would have been preferred.

The men on the buggy seat seemed to chatter incessantly.
Running Fawn wondered if white people ever stopped long
enough to make time for thinking. They laughed a lot too.
Hearty chuckles or loud guffaws. It made Running Fawn
nervous.

She wished she could get down and walk. The jostling
buggy had her bones aching. Besides, the dust from the wagon's wheels and hooves of the horses filled her eyes and her
nose, making her want to sneeze.

The sun beat down unmercifully. She wished she had a
hat like the men up front. She was tempted to place her small
bundle on her head, but she didn't want to be noticed or seen
in need of help.

She still had not spoken to Silver Fox. She felt angry with

him. Angry that he was such a good student. Angry that he didn't seem at all concerned about leaving their home and people. She was sure that her situation was due to his diligence. The strangers would not have picked her for the long journey had not Silver Fox done so well and gotten Man With The Book to think of Mission School for him. And they couldn't send just one from the small band. It would look like favoritism for the chief's son. But why couldn't it have been one of the boys? Or even Laughing Loon? She would not have minded leaving her family's campfire nearly as much as Running Fawn.

But it was not one of the boys, and it was not Laughing Loon. She, Running Fawn, was sitting on the buggy seat, forlornly watching the miles slip away beneath the wheels that lifted dust to settle on her dark buckskin skirts.

She had left her heart with her own people in the little community on the prairie that she knew and loved.

꙼   ꙼   ꙼

"Are you well?" It was the first that Silver Fox had spoken to her directly. He did not use the English words they had learned but spoke in their native tongue.

She turned to look at him. His face looked genuinely concerned.

Taking a break from the heat of the day, they sat side by side in the shade of some scrubby bushes near the edge of the Bow River that they generally had been following. It felt good to get out of the sun. It was good to hear the song of the flowing water. It had been good to kneel on the cool, damp ground and lift the cold wetness to splash on her flushed and dusty face.

The two men in the black coats had walked on along the river. She did not trouble herself to wonder where they were going—or if they were coming back.

She now turned away from Silver Fox. His question, asked kindly, threatened to bring the tears to her eyes. She shook her head slowly. She was not well.

"Did you not wish to come?" he continued.

For a moment Running Fawn felt that she would choke with emotion. She shook her head again.

There was heavy silence with only the distant call of a meadowlark to break the stillness.

"I am sorry," came the quiet response, and Running Fawn felt that the words were truly spoken.

She wished that she could get up and move away—but there really was no place to go. Besides, she ached so badly from all the jostling that she wished she would never need to move again.

"I wanted to," said Silver Fox in little more than a whisper.

Running Fawn favored him with a dark scowl. That was the whole problem. His desire to learn and learn.

"I want to study so that I can help my people," he continued.

Running Fawn made no reply.

"Someday I may be chief," he continued matter-of-factly, no bravado in his tone.

Running Fawn gave him another dark look. Of course he would be chief. His father was old. Chief Calls Through The Night would not be chief of their band for long.

"I want to be a wise chief," said Silver Fox, his eyes on some faraway object unknown to Running Fawn.

She twisted sharply to stare at him. "Your father is a wise chief," she responded hotly.

She did not need to say that his father had never been to the white man's school.

But Silver Fox did not seem perturbed by her outburst, only nodded.

For many moments they sat in silence and then he spoke again. Slowly. Softly.

"These are different times. It will never be the same again. If our people are to survive, to prosper, we must learn to live in the new world. With new ways."

"Would you forsake the old?" she demanded.

"No. No," he quickly answered. "We must build upon them. But we must move on. We must. I—"

But she had heard enough. In spite of her reluctance to leave the cool spot in the shade she sprang to her feet.

"The old ways are good," she spat at him. "There is no reason to leave them. I will not—will *not*—take the ways of the white man. I will not."

With her angry cry ringing in the air, she left him and ran along the riverbank until she rounded the bend and no longer was in sight. Exhausted by the heat and her emotions, she sunk into a little heap on the rich river grasses and let the sobs shake her entire body.

☙ ☙ ☙

Running Fawn had never seen so many wooden buildings intermingled with strange-looking tent dwellings in one area. They traveled through narrow passages lined with the structures, where people, mostly white people, hurried back and forth, always seeming determined to get to some other place.

Dust from the wheels of their buggy joined that of many other conveyances to fill the air and every available crevice.

She wanted to turn to Silver Fox and ask him if this was Fort Calgary, but she still was angry with him and would not speak.

At last the driver of the team pulled back on the leather straps and said a loud "whoa." The buggy rolled to a stop in front of a large white building.

"Here we are," announced the second man, looking back at them and giving them a big grin.

Running Fawn sat and stared. For some reason it was not at all what she had expected—though she could not have described what it was she had expected. It simply was all so strange. Where were the tepees? Where were the campfires? How did one ever—?

The man on her side of the buggy stretched long legs down toward the ground and eased himself slowly from the seat. He reached up a hand toward Running Fawn.

"Down with you," he said good-naturedly. "We are at journey's end."

Running Fawn knew he expected her to be happy with the news, but she could feel no joy.

She could feel Silver Fox stirring beside her. For one brief moment she wished to reach out and wrap her fingers in his buckskin shirt just as she used to do with her mother's skirts. But she turned from him instead and let the tall man help her over the wheel of the wagon.

And then she was being led down a rock-hard path with green grass on either side and flowers tucked in all together in tight clumps rather than scattered freely.

A large door opened before them and a white woman, flaming red hair piled high on her head and a dark dress trimmed with bits of white, stepped out. She was smiling. Running Fawn saw both white gentlemen sweep off their tall hats and bow slightly. Running Fawn wondered if that was the proper thing to do—but she had no hat. She ducked her head in a brief awkward bow.

"I see you have brought my new charges," said the woman with another smile.

"We have, Mrs. Nicholson," said the shorter of the two tall men.

"Well—do let me see them." She moved forward.

"We are so pleased to have you join our Mission School," she said in rapid English that was hard for Running Fawn to follow.

She reached for Running Fawn first, placing her hands gently on her shoulders and turning her to catch the last rays of the afternoon sun.

"You must be Running Fawn," she said pleasantly.

Running Fawn did not even nod in agreement. She wasn't sure what she was expected to do or say.

"Indeed she is," said the taller man and he gave Running

Fawn's arm a little nudge. "Say good day to your matron, Mrs. Nicholson."

Running Fawn concentrated hard.

"Goo'day your matron, Miz Niccason," she managed to repeat.

A loud guffaw followed her words.

Running Fawn swallowed hard and looked from one face to another. She did not know why one tall man had responded with the hearty laugh and the other had coughed and turned slightly away. The woman simply smiled and reached out a hand to Running Fawn's cheek. The whole scene made Running Fawn dreadfully uncomfortable. But the attention then turned to Silver Fox.

"And you are Silver Fox," the woman said and offered her hand to the young brave.

He accepted it, bowing ever so slightly as he said in a respectful, yet confident voice, "Good day, Mrs. Nicholson. So nice to meet you."

The red-haired lady beamed. It was plain that she was impressed with the young man.

"You must all be weary," she said, looking around the group. "Please come in. I've asked Miss Brooke to draw you a bath, Running Fawn, and then she will bring you some supper. And you, Silver Fox, one of our boys, Wilbur, will show you to your dormitory. There is a bath waiting for you as well."

And Running Fawn was whisked off down a long corridor, where another smiling lady waited to escort her farther into the depths of the enormously overwhelming white building.

❧   ❧   ❧

Running Fawn's first thought was that she would be led to a quiet stream, the only experience she had ever had with bathing. The strange words "draw you a bath" were totally confusing, but she fell into step with the woman whose hand rested lightly on her shoulder, and meekly allowed herself to be led away. For one brief moment she forgot her anger with Silver Fox and wished with all her heart that she did not need to leave him.

They entered a strange little room. Sitting on clawed feet against one wall was a very large, shining white basin, half-filled with water. Running Fawn stood and stared.

"I will leave you to have your bath, and then I will return to show you where to wash your hair," the woman said, still smiling.

"After you have washed thoroughly, you may wear these clothes." She indicated a stack of garments lying on a nearby wooden object that Running Fawn had already learned was a chair.

Running Fawn looked down at her own garments, a mixture of buckskins and white man's cotton.

"Just place your things in that basket," explained the woman, indicating the basket she intended.

She turned then and left the room with one more word. "Be sure you use lots of soap."

After the door had closed softly, Running Fawn just stood there and stared. First at the closed door, then the footed tub with its generous supply of water, and then down at the clothes she was to put on, then at her own that she was to leave in the woven basket. It was all so strange—this bath of the white man.

With trembling fingers she began to remove her clothing, still feeling unsure of just how one used the strange white object for one's bath. Tentatively she climbed over the side and stood in the middle of the tub. It was slippery under her feet and the water was very warm. Running Fawn was used to bathing in frigid waters. How could one be refreshed in water that did not even cool the body?

Standing in the middle of the slippery tub she began to splash the water over her torso. Soap—another commodity the white man had brought. She was to use lots of soap. She found a piece in the dainty dish by the side of the tub and began to generously lather her entire body. She had to whip up waves of water to rinse all the sweet-smelling suds away. It was even harder to stand upright when the sudsy mixture foamed about the slick enclosure.

At last Running Fawn was convinced that she had washed thoroughly. With a great deal of care and clinging to the side to keep from slipping, she managed to climb from the tub. The floor was wet with splashed water and little islands of soap suds. She found it very slippery, too.

She padded across the puddles and reached for the clothing on the chair, casting a longing look at the little pile of discarded garments in the basket to her right. She did wish that she could put her own things back on.

Reluctantly she unfolded the items before her. There were strange things in the pile. Running Fawn had no idea what they were or how they were to be worn. At last she came to the conclusion that the white woman had not meant for her to wear them all at one time. She began to shiver slightly as she pulled the shirtwaist over her wet arms and buttoned the tiny buttons with nimble yet nervous fingers. The task was new and strange. Then she pulled on the stockings, twisting the tops and tucking them under, as she had always done in the past. She gently laid aside the strange little garment with the long elastic tabs and funny little clips and placed it on the growing pile of unneeded articles. A girl she had met in the hallway had been wearing a white shirtwaist and a gray skirt. She reached for the gray skirt that looked just like it and let it drop over her head. The buttons were much larger and easier to fasten, but the skirt was too large for her. It sagged over her hips. But she was ready. Ready for the school mistress to show her what she was to do next. The shirtwaist and skirt were already showing patches of wetness as they sopped up the moisture from her body, but nothing could be done about that. There was no sun in the room to dry the excess water. She crossed her arms and waited silently, now and then casting a glance toward the soggy floor or the chair that still held several pieces of clothing that she had not needed.

At last the door opened. Running Fawn looked up—just in time to see Miss Brooke's face blanch even paler than it naturally was and hear a sharp intake of breath. Her arms lifted in unison and her eyes opened wide in shock. "Mercy me," was all that Running Fawn heard her say. The young girl had no idea what the words meant.

Chapter Nine

Lessons

From then on, everything was carefully explained to Running Fawn. It seemed that she was always being shown something. You hold it this way, you wear it like this, you use this for that, you put this here, place that there. On and on it went as she was introduced to the strange ways of the white man. Often she felt confused. Frustrated. Many times she wished to say, "It works better like this," but she never said the words. She wondered if Silver Fox was going through the same difficult initiation.

Though her days were trying and filled with frustrations, Running Fawn was able to muddle her way through, catching on quickly to the new information and experiences that continually presented themselves. She did not need to be shown something twice, but kept a careful eye on the actions and movements of the other girls. She knew they frequently tittered behind their hands at her expense, and though she really didn't care what they thought of her, the pride of the Blackfoot tribe was at stake.

It was the nights that were the most painful and lonely. Running Fawn did not allow herself to weep after the lights had been put out and the dormitory had finally settled down to soft breathing as others slept. But something deep within her seemed to curl up and die a little bit more with each passing day until she felt numb and drained of all emotion. All but the intense longing to leave this place and return home to her own people.

She saw very little of Silver Fox. The boys' dormitory was in a separate building from where the girls lived. The playgrounds too were divided by a large wooden fence. There were times that she caught glimpses of him as they sat in chapel or marched to the dining room. He looked very strange in the white man's clothes. A white shirt with a bit of dark cloth hanging down its front and gray flannel pants. She wondered if he hated the awkward, hard shoes as much as she did.

One of the most difficult adjustments was to the white man's unusual sleeping habits. They insisted, after her first night on the floor, that she use the odd frame they called a bed. She was to climb up on it, then slip into it, at just the right place, between this and that. The blankets were to be gently pulled up over her, not wrapped around her. She was to put her head on the soft whiteness they called a pillow. But it felt strange to her and kept tumbling to the floor throughout the night with all her tossing and turning.

There was no one to snuggle up against. All the other occupants of the room slept alone in beds just like hers. She had to warm the stiff white sheets with the heat from her own slender body, and some nights she shivered alone for hours before she could get to sleep.

Mealtimes at first had been another dreadful experience, but very quickly she learned how to hold the fork or spoon "properly" and get the food from her plate to her mouth. She sometimes wondered why she even bothered when some of the dishes were so lacking in flavor. She often longed for a good slice of venison roasted over an open fire or a piece of pemmican, with its tangy richness of dried buffalo meat and sun-ripened berries.

But in the classroom, Running Fawn found herself momentarily forgetting her uneasiness and discomfort. She loved this new world of learning. She loved the many books available to her. There was excitement in discovering the world in a totally new way. She plunged into the lessons with her total being and for an all-too-brief period each day could forget how much she longed to return home to her own people.

But as soon as the teacher announced, "Class dismissed," Running Fawn felt the sorrow and loneliness close in upon her again. Now she was back in the world of young white girls. They were noisy and pushy, and if a supervisor was not looking, often rude. They teased and ignored her by turn, snickering and pointing and raising eyebrows in silent messages. Running Fawn then wished with all her being that she could turn her back and walk away. Walk away forever.

☙ ☙ ☙

"Why don't you join the others?"

Miss Brooke asked the question of Running Fawn one sunny afternoon while the girls squealed their excitement and tossed a ball back and forth on the green grass of the playground. "Don't you like dodge ball?"

Running Fawn let her eyes travel back to the noisy circle. So that was dodge ball. She had made little sense of the game, but then, she had paid little attention.

She shook her head, then quickly added in soft accented English as she had been taught, "No, ma'am."

"I'm sure you would be good at it," went on Miss Brooke. "You are naturally athletic."

Running Fawn wasn't sure what "naturally athletic" was, though she had heard one of the teachers use the same words when speaking about Silver Fox. Perhaps it had something to do with being Indian.

She shook her head slowly.

"You do need exercise," went on the persistent Miss Brooke. "Come on. Let's both join the others."

She held out her hand and reluctantly Running Fawn allowed herself to be led over to the game.

"Make room," Miss Brooke said to the nearest girls. "We are joining you."

Running Fawn did not miss the frowns that spread quickly around the small circle.

"She doesn't know how to play," the girl named Molly, now holding the ball, dared to argue.

"Then we'll teach her," said Miss Brooke. She turned to Running Fawn. "The girls in the middle are 'it.' The object of the game is to hit one of them with the ball as you pass it back and forth around the circle. They try to keep from being hit. If the ball does touch one, that person must come out of the circle. The last girl left in the circle is the winner. Do you understand?"

Running Fawn had listened carefully. She understood and nodded.

They began the game again. At first the group showed little enthusiasm, but as the game progressed, the girls again picked up their squealing, and Running Fawn seemed to be forgotten.

The girls in the circle ran around and around, crying and calling and skipping lightly out of the path of the tossed ball. Running Fawn kept her eyes on the whole procedure. So far the ball had not come her way.

A small girl with light lemon braids was hit and had to join the outer circle. Then a girl named Meg, whom the girls in the dorm called Topper, was "out." As the game went on, Running Fawn's dark eyes riveted on the frisking, dodging Molly, one of the few still left in the middle.

And then the ball bounced her way. Before any of the other girls could move to retrieve it, Running Fawn snatched it up quickly and with one quick, hard delivery sent it careening straight at the unsuspecting older girl, hitting her in the chest with such force that it toppled her to the ground.

"Oh, my," she heard Miss Brooke exclaim as the woman hastily hurried forward to check on the fallen student.

Other than being shaken and angry, Molly was not injured. She got up, brushing at her gray skirt, eyes flashing as she cast a glance Running Fawn's way.

Miss Brooke, looking relieved that no serious harm had been done, turned back to Running Fawn. "We forgot to tell you that you just toss the ball gently," she said patiently. "And we throw the ball low. From the waist down. The waist down." She held her hand at her own waist and let it sweep downward to show the girl exactly what she meant. Running Fawn nodded mutely to let the woman know that she understood.

The woman lifted the little chain that she wore around her neck and looked at the small watch that dangled at the end.

"It's almost time to wash for supper," she said. "I think that's enough exercise for one day."

Running Fawn turned away from the little group and started for the dormitory washroom. She did not even glance at the other girls. But as she walked her dark eyes took on a shine. For once, just once, she had bested the big, bossy Molly.

❧   ❧   ❧

Besides the daily chapel times, there were religious instruction classes. Running Fawn felt a certain amount of curiosity about the white man's God, but she kept a careful inner distance from any deep interest. She knew instinctively that as long as she was at the school, she would not be allowed to sing the Blackfoot chants or do any dancing to the Sun God. But that did not trouble her, as she would not have felt inclined to do it on her own in any circumstance. The religion of her people was a joining together. She needed the rest of her band to take part in the ceremony. The Indian tradition was that only seeking the Great Spirit's vision was done alone in a quiet place of meditation. Running Fawn had not reached the age where she was encouraged by her tribal elders to take her own spiritual journey toward that vision.

So she drifted, feeling that while at the school she had no

connection with God, any god, in any way. She was an observer, apart. Merely looking on as the others went through their simple ceremony that involved no fire, no good medicine, no drums, and no dancing. There was singing, but it had little in common with the chants Running Fawn had grown up with and understood.

Everything seemed to be centered on the big Black Book. It looked much like the Black Book that the missionary had brought to Running Fawn's band, and Running Fawn heard many of the same words read from the Book. It seemed strange to her that both Black Books should carry the same words, until she realized that many of the books in the chapel and in the classrooms were also duplicates. That seemed to take away the mystery.

On most days, Running Fawn was content to lay all thought of worship aside. But on certain days, days when she looked at the turning leaves or heard the honking of the geese that passed overhead, she remembered that such events had significance for her people and would mean a ceremony would take place in the camp. On those days Running Fawn longed for home with renewed passion. She felt increasingly alone and lonely, shut away from her people and the life she had known and loved.

❧   ❧   ❧

An unusual amount of excitement swept along the corridors and throughout the classrooms. Something known as a *track meet* was to take place. Running Fawn had no idea what the excitement was all about, and she didn't suppose that she would care too much anyway. She decided to retreat to a corner of the large playground and let the girls chatter on in their noisy, high-pitched voices.

There was a good deal of activity in the field. For a moment Running Fawn let her eyes drift over the running to and fro of busy figures. She had never seen the white people running about with such animation. Perhaps there was to be a hunt. New structures had been raised here and there across the open field. Yet they did not look like corrals for rounding up mustangs, nor blinds from which to shoot wild game. They were not piskuns, the Blackfoot word for buffalo jumps. But then, that would be foolish. There were no more buffalo.

Running Fawn turned her back. Whatever it was, it was of no interest to her.

☙   ☙   ☙

In spite of her determination to remain aloof from the present events, Running Fawn felt her pulse quickening. The track meet had turned out to be a sporting event, and Running Fawn had always enjoyed the competitions held among her people when the young men and braves contended wholeheartedly in various events to prove their strength or valor. She found it hard not to be interested now, though many of the events were foreign to her and she could not understand the rules that governed the activities.

It was of particular interest to her when Silver Fox turned out to be one of the athletes. The other girls seemed to each pick a certain young man whom they cheered on noisily. No one was calling out the name of Silver Fox, who was now called Thomas by the members of the school. There were calls of "Run, Wilbur," or "Go, Carl," but she heard no urging on of the dark boy named Thomas.

Running Fawn, known in the school as Martha, did not call out his name either. But inwardly she gloried each time he bested the other boys. He was particularly skilled in running, and won most of the events in that sport. He also placed in the discus and outthrew all the boys with the javelin. Running Fawn felt pride—not personally, but for her people. Suddenly she felt challenged to prove her race superior. Perhaps she should not withdraw from the sports events. She was sure that she could do as well as the other girls. Maybe even better. Perhaps, for the sake of her people, she should become involved in the white man's sports. There was honor at stake. She should have realized it earlier. She would help Silver Fox uphold the dignity of their people.

❧   ❧   ❧

From then on Running Fawn allowed herself to be drawn into the games and physical activities. The girls soon realized that whenever she played, she played well and played to win. This was a matter that caused discord when they played against one another in their own schoolyard, but changed quickly whenever they played against another school. Then Running Fawn was not just pushed to the front and cheered on, she was expected to win for the student body. Then the honor was not hers—it was theirs. Running Fawn found the whole thing confusing. How could girls who normally turned their backs when she entered a room suddenly begin cheering loudly when she competed against other schools? It did not make a bit of sense to the young Indian girl.

Nor did she understand their anger when she occasionally failed to win one of those competitions.

"What happened? Why didn't you try harder? You could have won." These comments came her way on the playing field or in the quietness of the dorm later that night.

Running Fawn soon learned that though she may not have sought it, she had taken on the responsibility of representing their school in all sporting events. But inwardly she was not representing them, she was representing her people. When she won, it was for Blackfoot honor. When she failed to win, it was not because she had not given it her best. She would willingly die before she would disgrace her Indian blood—her heritage.

She did not attempt to explain this, for they would not have understood anyway.

❧   ❧   ❧

"You did really good."

The words were spoken by Marilee, a girl who shared Running Fawn's table at mealtime and dorm room at night. Apart from necessary polite exchanges, they had not spoken to each other, though the girl had offered tentative smiles on a few occasions. Marilee seemed as shy and withdrawn as Running Fawn herself, so the few brief words of affirmation after the track meet came as a suprise to the young Blackfoot.

Running Fawn's eyes lifted to the blue eyes before her. She saw the uncertain smile flicker briefly. She nodded in recognition of the compliment but did not respond further.

She was not sure of the meaning in those few words. Was the white girl simply making a statement—or offering friendship?

Running Fawn nodded again and paused for a moment to try to better understand the approach. Marilee did not move away.

"Would you like to play catch after supper?" the white girl asked, still in the same shyly quiet voice.

Running Fawn shook her head. "I have to work in the kitchen," she answered, relieved for the excuse. A look of disappointment filled the blue eyes.

As Running Fawn moved away she puzzled over the brief encounter. The girl seemed genuinely friendly. Perhaps, just perhaps, she should have been more responsive.

But even as the thought crossed her mind, she felt herself withdraw. She wasn't sure of the ways of the white people. Of the motives. She must be guarded. Must not reach out too eagerly. It was wise to be cautious.

❧   ❧   ❧

That evening Marilee offered Running Fawn a cookie from the box her mother had sent. Marilee had also offered a cookie to each of the other girls in the dorm room, and they exclaimed and smacked their lips in appreciation. Running Fawn inwardly longed to taste the treat, but she shook her head and retreated silently to her little bed and picked up the book she had brought from the library. As she did each night, she would read until it was time to turn the lights out.

She was quite aware of the good-natured chatter that went on in the room, but she tried hard to block it out.

When she peeked around the opened book, she saw the other girls lounging about the room in their long nighties as they chattered about frivolous things—all except for Marilee. Marilee was also already in her bed, her own book opened before her.

⚜   ⚜   ⚜

Over the days that followed, Running Fawn was invited to share various activities, not only by Marilee but from other girls as well. Running Fawn always carefully assessed each situation. If it was a game they were playing, a sporting event, she would gladly take part. If it was something of a more intimate nature, she declined with a shake of her head. Never did she feel comfortable entering into their light and lively conversations.

So she held herself apart—part of their world, but always an outsider. They seemed to accept her on her own terms. Including her in their playground activities, leaving her out of their girlish conversations.

Running Fawn could not have expressed it, but the shy yet warm smiles that Marilee sent her way were important to her well-being. She watched for them, and in her heart she considered the young girl her friend.

Chapter Ten

A Visitor

After what seemed like years of being away from her own people, the school term came up to the Christmas holidays. Running Fawn breathed a deep sigh of relief as she watched excited classmates pack their things in little rectangular valises and ready themselves for the arrival of their folks. Running Fawn couldn't understand all the fuss about Christmas, but she wished she could pack too. Her heart beat faster at the mere thought of seeing family and home again. She would be only too glad to leave behind the strange pale faces and jeers from the other girls along with the snowy white shirtwaists, gray pleated skirts, and unfamiliar undergarments.

She went looking for Miss Brooke to inquire about her own clothing, but it was Miss Brooke who found her instead.

"There you are," she said cheerily. "I've been looking for you. Mrs. Nicholson would like to see you in her office."

Perhaps she is going to tell me where to find my things, thought Running Fawn. She hurried after Miss Brooke, who was leading the way down the hall with long strides.

"Martha. Come in, my dear," Mrs. Nicholson greeted her. "Have a seat." She indicated the chair across the desk from her own.

Running Fawn knew this was more than the whereabouts of her possessions if she was to sit down. She did so woodenly, then lowered her head to stare at motionless hands in her lap.

"I suppose you have heard all the commotion about Christmas vacation?" asked Mrs. Nicholson.

Running Fawn nodded.

"We always take a bit of a break this time of year before starting second term."

Running Fawn did not even bother to nod again.

"We have decided that you and Silver Fox will stay on over Christmas. There really is no way to transport you— home, with winter storms being so unpredictable and all. . . ." Her voice trailed off as Running Fawn sat motionless.

The woman smiled pleasantly, not seeming to notice the alarmed expression in Running Fawn's eyes, as she continued. "Staff will care for you here. They are all quite willing to share the responsibility. This will be new for us. We have never had students stay over the holiday before. But . . . it seems to be the best solution."

Running Fawn slowly looked up from the fingers in her lap. *No,* her mind shouted, *no, it isn't the best. I want to see my people. My mother. She will have a new baby by now. I haven't seen it. I don't even know if it is a boy or a girl. I need to go home. I need to.*

But she did not speak. She merely nodded her head, while her heart broke with longing to return home to those she loved.

Mrs. Nicholson's smile widened. "Well, then," she said, "I guess it is all cared for." She stood, indicating the interview was concluded.

Running Fawn struggled to her feet and left the room without so much as a further glance at the head matron. There was nothing she could say or do. She allowed herself to be shepherded back to her dorm room, now vacant of other girls.

"We will be able to teach you all sorts of special chores over the vacation time," Miss Brooke enthused. "Mrs. Nicholson said that I might show you how to do the laundry and polish the silverware."

Running Fawn did not respond. Miss Brooke added, "And if things go well, they might even let you learn to use the sewing machine."

Running Fawn tried hard to swallow away the lump that persisted in trying to choke her. Miss Brooke was trying to cheer her, she realized that—but nothing could take away her deep hurt in being kept from her people.

🙵   🙵   🙵

When spring rolled around and the students were getting ready to leave for the summer months at term end, Running Fawn was a bit more prepared when she was called to Mrs. Nicholson's office again. The story was the same. It was wisest for her and Silver Fox to stay on. There would be special lessons, just for them, over the summer months. Advanced work for Silver Fox to bring him up to the standard of the boys his own age who had been in school since their early years, and lessons in homemaking for Running Fawn. Sorrowfully she conceded, though she could not keep her eyes from drifting frequently to the southeast. Somewhere out there on the plains, her people lived. She wondered if they even remembered her or if she had been totally forgotten, totally given to the white man's world.

🙵   🙵   🙵

"Hello." The one word of greeting was spoken in English, and then the speaker repeated the greeting in the Blackfoot language. Running Fawn's head came up. It was so long since she had heard the soft, melodic tones of her native tongue.

Silver Fox stood before her, a wooden-handled hoe in his hands.

"So we are to keep the garden," he commented. "That is

good. When we return you will know more about making the plants grow."

The brief reference to the little garden Running Fawn had planted on the Reserve both pleased and upset her. For some reason, she was glad that Silver Fox remembered her small plot of ground, yet saddened as she thought again of its loss along with everything else that was important to her.

She nodded now and turned back to her weeding.

"Do you like working the garden?" he persisted.

"Better than working the iron," replied Running Fawn shortly. She looked up quickly and caught a smile on his lips.

"It is silly work, the ironing," hissed Running Fawn. "Why take out the wrinkles with a hot iron in the heat of the day, when they will be back as soon as the clothes are worn?"

Silver Fox laughed outright.

He laid the hoe on the ground and knelt down to Running Fawn's level. For a time he was silent, lifting handfuls of fine soil and letting it sift through his open fingers.

"Do you like it here, now?"

The personal question, spoken in a low and guarded manner, made Running Fawn wonder how much he knew, how much he had guessed about her feelings.

She slowly shook her head, not raising her eyes to his.

The silence settled between them. Running Fawn kept on with her weeding.

At length he spoke again. "I want to learn as much as I can. This is a new world. I do not want my people to . . . to be left behind. We can help them—with our knowledge. We can teach them how to survive—without the buffalo. We can bring them medicines. Food. Implements for farming. They can only use them—if they have the knowledge."

He was so earnest that Running Fawn could not any longer refrain from looking into his face—his fathomless dark eyes. He really meant his words, she could see that, and for the moment he convinced her that he was right. She longed to believe that these days of loneliness and sacrifice would bring something of benefit to her people.

The face of Silver Fox was intense, the flashing dark eyes filled with passion. She wanted to believe him—whatever he spoke.

"Running Fawn," he said, and the use of her Indian name sounded sweet to her ears, like she had just been given back a very part of herself, "we are the first ones to go to school. We need to prove that we can be students—learn. So we can teach—our people."

She nodded silently. Perhaps he was right. Perhaps they had a duty to perform. A duty toward their people.

But she hoped with all her heart that the days would pass quickly. She was so anxious to go home.

ᵛᵛ   ᵛᵛ   ᵛᵛ

In the fall three more Indian students were brought to the school. They were from the Blood tribe, but all part of the larger Blackfoot Nation. There were two boys whom she gave little attention and one girl, slightly younger than herself. Running Fawn did not recognize them from any of their joint campsites in the past.

Running Fawn could see in the young girl's eyes the same fears, the same confusion that she herself had felt when she first entered the doors of the school. But by now she could go through all the proper motions, doing her work and living her life, taking her place at the table and sleeping in the white-sheeted bed, as though she had been living in such a manner all her life. Inwardly, though, she had never totally adjusted. She held a certain resentment toward the white man. Her ways were just as good. No—in many instances, they were better. Much better. Not so rigid, so confining. One could breathe more easily, walk more quietly, stand with greater comfort in the clothing of her people. And one could sleep much more soundly bundled in warm wool blankets and buffalo robes, snuggled up against the back of another family member. She still didn't care much for some of the ways of the white man.

When introduced to the new girl, who would be called Esther, she stepped forward and held out a welcoming hand. She did not want the trembling youngster to go through the same fearful experiences that she herself had faced. The very first thing she would do when they were alone would be to explain to the young girl how white people took a bath.

March 16, 1884

Dear Christian Brothers,

I have cause for great rejoicing but also deep heaviness of heart. There has finally been a spiritual breakthrough, at least to some degree. Five believers are now meeting at my humble dwelling for Sunday Bible study and worship. However, they do come with some trepidation, as their chief still has not made known whether he favors the action. If only he would take a stand for the Gospel! I am sure most of his people would follow.

For these few, I am most thankful to God. I feel confident now that in the near future the rest of the band will understand the message that I seek to bring.

There have been good reports, both in academics and deportment, from the boarding school where our two best students are in attendance. They also have done well in the sports activities, but they still seem hesitant to embrace the Gospel. We must be diligent in prayer on their behalf.

But the greatest concern for me at the moment is the health of my people. It seems that the last few months have brought one epidemic after another. First whooping cough passed through the entire Reserve, taking many of the young and a few of the elderly as well. Then, when the people were most unable to resist, influenza struck, taking many more. Now we realize that we are in the midst of a fight against tuberculosis. In spite of the efforts of the Agent and help from the

North West Mounted Police, there is little in the way
of medicine. We have used up all our supplies, and so
much more is needed. I have done what I could, nursing those where I am able and giving out the little bit
of rations and cures that I am able to obtain, but it is
so little against such a great need.

I have now decided that I must make a trip to the
city to see if I can find some help for the people. It will
not be an easy undertaking, as the spring winds are
still bringing in periodic snowstorms and traveling is
difficult. Two Hawk, one of the young men from the
tribe, has said that he is willing to travel with me, and
the chief is allowing me the use of one of his horses. I
will leave at sunup.

Your humble servant,
Martin Forbes

⇛   ⇛   ⇛

"Martha," Miss Brooke said, coming into the kitchen
where Running Fawn helped prepare the evening meal, "you
have a visitor. Mrs. Nicholson says you are to be excused
from your duties to go to her office."

Running Fawn untied her apron and hung the checkered
covering on the hook provided. A frown creased her usually
smooth brow. Who would be coming to see her? Was Silver
Fox asking for some kind of meeting? But why?

As she entered the room she noticed that it was a white
man who occupied the chair across from Mrs. Nicholson. A
white man she did not know. He stood to his feet when she
entered the room, a slight smile lighting his face.

"Running Fawn," he greeted her in her own tongue. "You
have grown."

Running Fawn stared at the man. It was the missionary.
He was so thin that his garments hung loosely on his tall
frame. He had grown a beard, and his face looked older—
older and darkened, and there was a sadness in the blue eyes
that once had glinted with enthusiasm.

Running Fawn stood at the entrance to the room, taking in his appearance, trying to hold back a rush of questions about her people. He turned back to the matron and spoke again, his words in the language of the Blackfoot.

"May Running Fawn and I have some time together, please?"

The woman looked confused. "I'm afraid you must speak to me in English," she answered, and the man flushed and begged her pardon.

"Please," he repeated in English, "is there a place where I might talk with Running Fawn and Silver Fox?" he asked the woman.

"Certainly. Miss Brooke, show the Reverend to the library office. I'll send Thomas in to join you, Reverend, as soon as he arrives."

"Thank you, matron," the man acknowledged with appreciation.

Running Fawn turned to follow Miss Brooke to the small office the matron had indicated. The missionary paused a moment more.

"I do hate to impose, matron," he said in an apologetic tone, "but we have much to speak of. Would it be a dreadful inconvenience for our meal to be sent to the office as well?"

For one moment the matron looked unsure, then she smiled pleasantly and nodded. "I'll have a tray brought to you," she agreed.

"Thank you," the missionary replied. "I would hate to delay your supper hour or cause disruption in the dining room."

The matron nodded.

As soon as they had been shown to the library office, the missionary switched back to the tongue of the Blackfoot.

"How are you, Running Fawn?" His voice held such care that she wanted to weep.

"I . . . I am doing well." With head lowered.

"You have grown. You look so different . . . in the . . . the school uniform."

"I feel different." She raised her eyes to meet his penetrating gaze. He did not speak further for a time while he searched her face.

"Has it been difficult?" His words were gentle. She again lowered her gaze to stare down at her stiff leather shoes laced above her ankles. She did not speak. It was not necessary.

"I'm sorry," he said in a whisper. "I hoped it would . . . be all right for you . . . here."

The door opened quietly and Miss Brooke ushered Silver Fox into the room to join them. The young man greeted him joyfully.

"Look at you," exclaimed the missionary, pushing the young man back to arm's length and measuring him with his eye. "You are nearly as tall as I."

Silver Fox nodded, his smile full of quiet pride.

"How is school?"

"I am learning much." The reply came in English. Running Fawn wondered if Silver Fox now despised his native tongue, had forgotten it, or was merely showing off for the benefit of the white man.

"Good. Good."

But then Silver Fox quickly switched back to his own language. Maybe the one reply had simply been a subconscious response to a white man.

"How are things with our people? Do you have any news?" The questions quickly poured out, one on the heels of the other. "Are they keeping well? My father? Is he well? Have the people learned to make good crops?" With each new query, the eyes of the missionary seemed to darken.

"I do not bring . . . good news," he finally said when Silver Fox stopped for breath.

At the expression that crossed the face of the young man, he hurried on. "Your father is well. I saw him just before I left. He sent greetings.

"Others have not fared so well," the missionary explained after Silver Fox looked relieved. "That is why I have come to the city. To find medicine to take back to our people. There has been much sickness. Much."

Running Fawn, who had been quietly observing the exchange, suddenly stepped forward, fear gripping her heart.

"My mother?" she asked through stiff lips.

The missionary turned to her, his expression full of surprise.

"You have not heard?" He looked at her with deep concern and sympathy. She could only stare at him.

"I am sorry," was all he said.

The iciness within her crept upward, numbing her, chilling her very being. She could not move, could not speak. She was aware that the eyes of the missionary and Silver Fox were both fastened on her, but she could not respond.

"I am sorry," the missionary said again in a whisper, and his hand reached out to rest on her shoulder.

Silver Fox finally asked the questions she could not form. "When?"

"With the first snows of winter."

"What happened?"

"She was not strong. The new baby became sick with the whooping cough. She could not save him. Then she also took the illness."

So the new baby had been a boy. Her mother would have been so proud to have borne another son. A new flood of sorrow passed through her.

"And her father?" asked Silver Fox.

"He mourns."

Silver Fox nodded.

"Crooked Moose—and Little Brook. And Bright Star?"

"Crooked Moose and Little Brook are well."

So she also had lost her little brother, her mother's little pet, in the epidemic. She felt that she could not bear the pain that filled her spirit.

"Little Brook has her own fire," went on the missionary. Running Fawn lifted her eyes at the news that her sister had moved to another's tepee.

"Who?" asked Silver Fox with interest. "Who has won her hand?"

Man With The Book smiled. "He is from one of the other bands," he informed them. "They met at the well. He was watering his horses. She was drawing water for the cooking pot. His name is Tall Man."

There was a sound at the door, and young Esther brought in the tray with their supper.

Running Fawn tried to take a bit of the meal but found it hard to swallow. She sat and toyed with her food, pushing it back and forth on her plate while the missionary and Silver Fox continued to talk as they ate. She wished she could give her plate to the missionary. He looked like he could make good use of additional nourishment.

Running Fawn's mother was gone. Her little brother Bright Star and the baby brother she had never seen. Little Brook was now another's wife. Caring for her own fire, her own cooking pot. Who was looking after her father in his sorrow? Running Fawn felt a grief that she could not have expressed. And no one seemed to fully understand her feeling of loss, or the intense homesickness that overcame her heart.

Chapter Eleven

Striking Out

All the students had gone home for the summer months except the Indian young people. Little Flower—Esther as she had been named by the faculty—had left earlier because of illness. Mrs. Nicholson feared that she might be coming down with something communicable, and had her taken home by one of the school's staff. Running Fawn secretly thought that the real problem with the young girl was homesickness. This "disease of the heart" she could understand.

The two young boys who had joined the school that year seemed to be doing fine. Silver Fox had introduced them to dormitory life, and they also worked in the gardens and looked to be quite settled. Running Fawn kept to herself. Her grief over the loss of her mother and brothers was buried deep in her soul, and the fact that her father had no one to care for him, to prepare his food, to carry water for his needs, nagged at her.

Man With The Book had been successful in his mission to obtain more medicine for the Reserve. He had canvassed the city—doctors' offices in particular—and managed to put together a substantial supply. Armed with the drugs and as much food as he could gather, he hired a wagon and left again for the Reserve. Running Fawn ached to go with him but dared not voice her request.

Running Fawn looked forward to resuming her responsibilities in the garden, but before she could take up her trowel she was informed that with three boys to care for the garden, her help would not be needed there. She would work in the kitchen honing her cooking skills.

She was also assigned ironing duties. Although she did not like the task, she did a fine job of pressing cotton shirts and bed linens. She became so adept that she was even advanced to some of the finer clothing of the ladies on the staff.

The hot days of summer monotonously followed each other like matching beads on a string. Running Fawn had little to look forward to with the dawning of each new day. The three boys had one another's company and spent many hours tossing a ball or playing on the tennis courts, a sport they all were beginning to enjoy. Running Fawn was alone, except for staff women who were much her senior. When she finished the day's assignments there was little to fill the time until the next day began.

"Martha, you need something to fill your evening hours," Miss Brooke kindly observed one day. "Would you like some needlework?"

Running Fawn was not particularly interested in needlework. At least not the type the white ladies busied themselves with as they sat by their fire in the evenings. She shook her head.

"Would you like to read? I am sure Mrs. Nicholson wouldn't object to your using the library."

The thought was a pleasing one and Running Fawn was quick to seize it. "Reading would be nice," she agreed.

From then on the key to the library was placed where Running Fawn had access to it. Night after night she spent her hours with books.

"Running Fawn."

The young girl lifted her head and looked for the voice that spoke her Indian name.

"Over here." Silver Fox stood beneath the porch where Running Fawn sat with her book on her lap. She acknowledged his presence with a slight nod.

"I've news from the village," he continued.

Running Fawn stood quickly to her feet, her book forgotten in her hands.

"What news?" she asked eagerly as she took the steps down to the sidewalk.

"How did you get news?" she continued as she advanced toward Silver Fox.

"Eagle Claw was here. He just came from the Reserve. Man With The Book is ill. My father sent Eagle Claw for medicine."

"What is wrong?" asked Running Fawn, and was surprised at how deeply the information troubled her. Hearing of his illness, she realized just how much he had tried to help her people.

"They do not know. My father wanted him to go to a white man's doctor, but he is too ill to travel."

Running Fawn could not find words to respond. She knew that if the young missionary died, the band would indeed bear a great loss.

"Has Eagle Claw returned to our village?"

"Yes, he started back immediately."

"Why . . . why did he come here?" asked Running Fawn.

"To inform the mission. My father said that the white missionary needed his own people to pray. Perhaps the Great God of the white man would choose to spare him."

Running Fawn's eyes widened in astonishment. "Do you believe that?" she asked.

"I do not know," answered the young man slowly. "Perhaps." He hesitated. "Sometimes I think it is so—that the white man's God is real. Is right. And then I wonder."

Deep in thought for a while, at last he spoke again.

"If they are right," he observed carefully, "then our traditions—our beliefs about the spirit gods—are wrong."

"Our people are not wrong," she contested hotly. "We have

served the same gods for generations. They would not leave us now."

"Perhaps they already have," Silver Fox said, lowering his gaze sadly.

He then lifted his eyes to her face. "Eagle Claw also had another message," he said, and she noticed a softness in his voice. "One I was to bring to you."

Running Fawn waited.

"I'm sorry. Your father also is ill."

꙳   ꙳   ꙳

"I must go to my father," Running Fawn said, her voice quiet yet determined.

"I'm sorry. I know how you must feel, and I wish . . . I wish there was some way for us to get you home. But the men are all away right now. There is no one to take you to the Reserve. I'm sorry," said Mrs. Nicholson.

"I can go—"

"Oh no. You must not even think of such a thing. The trail is long and difficult—even for a man with horses. You would never make it alone."

"Please . . . please . . . perhaps Silver Fox would travel with me."

"That wouldn't be at all proper."

Proper? Running Fawn could not understand why traveling back to their own people would not be proper.

"The menfolk will be back in a week or so. We will see what can be done then," comforted Mrs. Nicholson. "Perhaps by then your father will be well again and the long trip will not be necessary."

Perhaps by then he will be dead, was Running Fawn's silent but desperate response.

"I have been told that another supply of medicines has just been procured for the Reserve," the lady added. "Your father will be in good hands. Reverend Forbes—"

"Reverend Forbes is also ill," cut in Running Fawn, her

agitation making her careless about her manners.

"Reverend Forbes? Oh, my. How ill?" said the woman, concern in her face.

"Very ill," responded Running Fawn. "Chief Calls Through The Night sent one of the men for medicine."

"Oh, my," said the woman again. "We must have special prayers—"

"Yes—I was to tell you. Silver Fox brought the word. The chief wished for the mission to pray."

"Does that mean that the chief has become a believer?" asked Mrs. Nicholson, enthusiasm in her voice, though concern still showed in her expression.

"A believer?"

"In God."

Running Fawn shook her head. "We have our own gods," she replied evenly.

"But—" began the woman and then stopped. Running Fawn knew she was a big disappointment to the faculty. In spite of their teaching, their prayers, their earnest desires, she would not accept their God.

Running Fawn turned to go, her head up proudly.

"Martha," the woman called softly after her.

Running Fawn turned slightly, her head still up.

"Do you . . . do you mind if we include your father . . . in our prayers?" the woman asked gently.

For one moment Running Fawn stared at the face of the woman. She saw only love and concern there. Not contempt or ridicule. At last she nodded.

"If you wish," was all she said as she left to go to her room.

All through the long hours of the night and into the next day, Running Fawn worried about her father, her thoughts circling back to the same place. She should be there. She should. He needed her to care for him. He did not even have the help of the missionary. The white man also was sick. Why did this strange man stay with her people? Why had he not left them after the buffalo were no longer? After all the illnesses had smitten the little band? Why had he not gone back to his own—to the comforts of the white man's lodge?

It was a puzzle to Running Fawn. She knew she would not stay with the white man if the situation were reversed. Were she free to go, she would leave immediately. Without a moment's hesitation.

I am free, came the startling thought. *I am not a prisoner. I am not bound. I can go. I will go!*

Running Fawn's head whirled into motion with plans. She needed supplies—yet she had nothing, and she would not steal. She really did not know the way—she would have to count on her instincts alone to guide her. She could not run off with the clothing that belonged to the school—yet she did not know where her own had been taken, and if she had them they doubtless would no longer fit. She had been a much younger, smaller girl when she had been brought to the boarding school almost two years earlier.

What could she do?

At last she concluded the only thing was for her to borrow from the school. She would leave a note, explaining her dilemma. She would promise to pay back her debt at the earliest opportunity. Surely there would be some way to clear her obligation in the future. She could not wait for the men to return. She had to get to her father.

Late that night Running Fawn stripped the pillowcase from her pillow and crept soundlessly toward the kitchen. The first thing she placed in her makeshift sack was a length of kitchen cord. She had no thongs to help her with her journey, so the cord would have to do. She placed a small loaf of bread in the pillowcase. Only one—she would allow herself no more. She sliced one wedge of cheese, carefully noting the portion size. She should have meat for strength on the journey, but there was none that was properly prepared. The cheese would have to do. After hiding the case with its contents in the bushes by the rear entrance, she returned to her room and took one blanket from the bed, then sat down to write her note to the matron.

"Please forgive me," the note said, "but I must see my father. He needs me. I cannot wait. I will pay you back for all that I have taken as soon as I am able." Following the statement was an itemized listing of all that she had that was not properly hers. The list was a lengthy one. She included the oxford shoes, the white shirtwaist, and the gray skirt.

Quickly she changed her mind and hurried to remove the school uniform she was wearing, arranging the blanket about her body in a long, loose robe. She would need the shoes, she decided. Her feet no longer were used to the hard rocks of the trails. She scratched the clothing items from her list, glad that she would not have so much to repay at a later date. Carefully folding the articles that were to be left behind, she laid them on her empty bed. She wished she would have had time to wash and iron each piece, but she could not delay her departure. Casting a last glance about the room, she left as quietly as the hard-soled shoes would allow.

Once outside the building, she retrieved her case and its food supply from the bushes and started off. Overhead the moon dipped in and out of scattered clouds. She wished she had its continual light to help her on her way. She needed to get her bearings. To decide how best to untangle herself from the streets of the city. Once in the open, she was sure she would be able to find her way home.

She was not sure of the path she should take, nor how many days she would be on the trail, but she was sure of one thing. She was going home.

It seemed to take forever for her to put the maze of criss-crossing streets behind her, but at last she was out on the open prairie. By the time she passed the last buildings and turned her face eastward, the morning sun was beginning to scatter bits of pink and gold across the distant horizon. She felt more confident now. The rising sun was just where she had expected it to be. With long, steady strides she set out in a southeasterly direction. That was where the Reserve and her village lay. There she would find her father—if she was in time.

She had not gone far when the shoes began to cut into her feet. What had seemed reasonably comfortable as she walked the halls or worked in the kitchen now became most uncomfortable. One spot on her heel was burning dreadfully.

I wish I had some moccasins, she found herself thinking over and over. But she did not have moccasins, nor any other footwear, except the pinching shoes that now rubbed and bruised with each step she took.

She wished she had left them in the room with the other garments. Now she would be obligated to repay something that had proved useless to her.

She bent over, undid the laces, and slipped her feet from the confining leather. But she could not simply discard them. Not yet. Perhaps she could simply return them when she repaid her debt. Maybe they would just accept them back rather than requiring a replacement pair.

She tossed them into the pillowcase that she carried. It made the load heavier as she lifted it to her shoulder, and again she wished she had left them back at the dormitory.

In the afternoon she saw riders coming toward her. At first she dared hope that they might be from her people, but they did not need to get too close before she realized they were not. Cowboys. Men from one of the many ranches that had sprung up in the area. She knew instinctively that she did not wish to meet them, so she altered her course.

The detour added more miles to her already long journey. But at least her trek through the draw and off the main track offered a bit of coolness from the hot afternoon sun. She dared not travel that direction for long, lest she become confused and lose her bearings. As soon as she was sure the riders had passed her by, she sought out the southeasterly course again, correcting the diversion by keeping an eye on the sun overhead.

Chapter Twelve

Persistence

There was much concern when Miss Brooke discovered the note left behind on Running Fawn's bed along with the little pile of school clothing.

The first decision was to send for Silver Fox to ask his counsel.

"Do you think she will realize it is too far and turn back?" asked Mrs. Nicholson in great agitation.

Silver Fox shook his head. He knew Running Fawn would not return. "She will go home," he said solemnly.

"But she will never manage it. A girl—alone. Such a long way with no provisions but . . . but a small loaf of bread and a slice of cheese. Oh, I wish she had taken more. I wish . . . We must pray that she—"

"She will be fine," said Silver Fox, though in his heart he knew the journey home would cost her dearly.

"I wish the men were here," said Mrs. Nicholson, wringing her hands.

Silver Fox spoke again, determination edging his voice. "I will go," he said quietly.

Mrs. Nicholson quickly swung around to face him. "Do you think you can find her? Will you be able to catch up to her?"

He nodded.

"Oh, please, then. Take supplies. Go after her. I'm so worried. Bring her back."

Silver Fox shook his head.

"No. I will not bring her back. I will take her home." He did not wait for any further response but went to his room to prepare for the trip.

☙   ☙   ☙

By the time Silver Fox returned, dressed in clothing more suitable for the trail than his white shirt and gray flannels, Mrs. Nicholson was anxiously standing on the porch, a large canvas bag of supplies at her feet.

"We have your provisions ready." Her words tumbled over each other.

Silver Fox nodded, then dropped down on one knee to quickly sort through the bundle. Two piles began to appear. One grew much more rapidly than the other.

"Could I have some matches, please?" he asked. "A sharp knife—and string—sturdy string—and a canteen with water. I will need a rifle and some shells—and one more blanket."

Mrs. Nicholson gestured toward Miss Brooke, who ran to collect the additional items.

Silver Fox gathered the small pile together and returned them to the bag.

"Thank you," he said, standing to his feet. He nodded toward the large pile of hastily sorted provisions that still lay on the porch. "I will not need those," he said simply.

"But—"

"They will slow my travel."

Mrs. Nicholson nodded.

Miss Brooke returned, out of breath from scurrying. "I have sent Otis for the gun," she explained as she thrust the other items toward the young man.

"A horse," exclaimed Mrs. Nicholson. "You will need a horse."

Silver Fox was surprised. It was one thing for them to give generously of their supplies. It was quite another for them to offer a horse. Especially one of the fine animals that Silver Fox had groomed when he had his turn at the barns.

"I know nothing of horses. You choose. And a saddle. Help yourself," encouraged Mrs. Nicholson.

"I will not need a saddle, thank you," replied Silver Fox. "But a horse would speed my travel."

Otis, the elderly groundskeeper, arrived with a fine-looking Winchester and a small bag of shells. "Six or eight will do," said Silver Fox.

"Take them all," cried Mrs. Nicholson. "Take them. You may need them."

Silver Fox was tempted to argue but there wasn't time. He nodded politely instead and placed the shells with his bundle.

"Otis, help him with a horse," commanded Mrs. Nicholson, still distraught. "Oh, I should have listened. I should have known how she was feeling. If anything happens to Martha, I will never forgive myself."

Miss Brooke slipped a comforting arm around the older woman's waist.

Silver Fox reached up to tip his school-supplied hat, nodded politely, and again expressed his thanks.

Then he laid the formal hat carefully on the porch bench. He would not need it on the trail. A rancher's Stetson would have been far more suitable for the ride ahead, but one was not available.

"May God go with you," Mrs Nicholson called after him as he left with Otis to select a horse.

Silver Fox turned one last time and lifted a hand to the two ladies who stood together on the porch. Miss Brooke was wiping tears with a cambric handkerchief, while Mrs. Nicholson held her hands tightly before her as though in prayer.

For the first time, Silver Fox genuinely hoped they were right. That the God they served really was as powerful as they claimed—and that He cared.

All through that first long day she traveled, stopping once to drink from a stream and eat a small piece of the bread with cheese. Her stomach growled and her burning feet complained at the rough treatment. The hot prairie sun overhead beat down upon her with dizzying relentlessness. But she had no intention of stopping any more than she absolutely had to. She would walk until darkness fell, and if the moon should light her way, she would continue to walk throughout the night as well.

It was early evening before she stopped again. But it was not for long. A shallow pond provided water to quench her thirst. She drank long and deeply and bathed her painful feet.

A lone coyote bayed out its lonely cry and another answered from a ridge to her right. Coyotes. She smiled. Where there were coyotes there were also other small animals. When her meager food supplies ran out, she would pursue other nourishment possibilities.

The half moon rose in the sky to the east. Running Fawn greeted it with thankfulness in her heart. She could keep on traveling in spite of aching back and legs and the stiffness in her shoulders, though the pack she carried was small. She shivered and pulled the blanket closer about her. A sharp wind blew out of the west, making her cold since the sun had gone down. All but her swollen feet. Her feet burned so badly she had to force one step after the other. If only she had some skins. Even bits of moss. But there was nothing she could do to protect her feet from the rocks and sharp grasses of the trail.

Toward morning she found another stream and drank again. It helped to ease her hunger pangs to fill her stomach with cool water. She lowered herself to the bank and pushed her feet under the surface until they reached into the soft mud. She wished there were some way that she could take the soothing mud along with her. She was tempted to tear a piece from the blanket and wrap her feet with muddied strips, but she quickly decided that she should not damage it. The boarding school would want their own blanket returned.

Again she journeyed on. She would walk as long as she could before the heat of the day overtook her. Then she would find a cool place in the gentle hills and lie down for a rest in the shade of the stubby shrubs.

꙳   ꙳   ꙳

She slept longer than she had intended. She roused herself, shook some of the pain from her aching muscles, and picked up her small pack. She was sorry to see that the sun had moved quite a distance toward the west.

The wind that had blown the night before had long since quieted, leaving the whole world stifling under dancing heat waves that shimmered over the brown prairie grasses.

For a moment, Running Fawn felt dizzy. She wondered if she had lost her way. But as she shaded her eyes against the sun and judged the time of day, she knew again the way she must travel. Home was somewhere beyond those distant southeasterly hills.

꙳   ꙳   ꙳

The rays of the hot sun streamed to earth with no mercy, and Silver Fox found himself wishing that he had kept the flimsy hat. Anything to protect his head.

He had no doubt that Running Fawn was somewhere ahead of him. How far had she traveled? What time during the night had she left? How much had she rested since being on the trail?

Miss Brooke had reported that she wore the oxfords. She would not be able to travel fast in the clumsy shoes. Nor would her feet hold up in them for long, he reasoned. Oxfords with no protective stockings would soon begin to form blisters.

He was sure that her sense of direction would take her toward the village as the crow flies. Many miles had been added when they had traveled with the men from the mission in the buggy, zigzagging across the prairie to stay in touch with settlers or ranchers. But Running Fawn would not be confused by that. She would not try to backtrack their original journey and would head directly for home.

The prairie swept in all directions for miles and miles. There were few farms and ranches and even fewer towns. She would need water. He had the canteen. Running Fawn did not. Would she follow the curving river to be sure that she had water? It would add miles to her journey.

So Silver Fox faced a decision. Should he turn his horse directly toward the distant campsite of his people or should he follow the rambling river as it generally made its way southeasterly?

He turned his horse toward the river, determining to follow the winding stream for some miles and check for signs along that bank that the girl had been there. If there was no indication that she had traveled the riverbanks, he could then adjust his course.

❧   ❧   ❧

Running Fawn entered a shallow draw and knelt in the shade of some small saskatoon bushes that offered some escape from the hot midday sun. She lifted her bread and cheese from the small bundle. The supply was already getting low, even though she had carefully rationed her daily intake. The bread was now dry and crumbly, and the cheese was becoming moldy and strong-smelling from the heat.

She broke off a small portion of each and ate the pieces slowly. She had already stopped to drink from the river just down the slope from where she rested.

If only I didn't have to keep going off course to find water, she thought to herself. *It would be much faster if I could just keep walking directly. I should have thought to bring a canteen or a bottle or some sort of container.*

But she hadn't thought. In their band's travels they made sure that they were never too far from a water source.

She finished her scant meal and reached up to loosen her hair. Now that she was not at the school she allowed her long, shiny black braids to hang over her shoulders instead of pinning them up in Miss Brooke's judgment of proper fashion.

But the braids had become disarrayed. Nimbly her fingers plaited them again and wound round the bit of hair she had taken from her own head to tie the ends.

It was so hot. So unmercifully hot. And the way was so long.

She lifted shaded eyes to the blazing sky and blinked at its brightness.

There in the sky was her god. The white people at the boarding school had much to say of the Christian God and His love. Did her god love her? If so, he had a strange way of showing it. There was no mercy being shown to her on this day. And her journey must be hastened. If she did not get home quickly she might never see her father again.

Running Fawn felt her heart quake within her. She had to be on the trail. But she was so weary. So weary. She would first take just a little rest and allow her burning feet to cool.

❧   ❧   ❧

Silver Fox had found no sign of Running Fawn. He decided to leave the river and head in a direct line toward the Reserve. Perhaps he should have done that to begin with. First he would need to rest his horse. The animal was sweaty and tired from the long hours in the burning sun.

He wondered if he should have brought the horse. He could have pushed on had he been on foot. But he could not disregard the weariness of the animal.

He had tried to pick wisely, choosing instead of the prancing thoroughbreds a rangy little pony that had been used as a dray animal. It was not particularly attractive but it looked solid and, he hoped, would have endurance. Now as he slipped from its back, he wondered if he should have left the little roan in the stable.

He ran a hand over its sweating side, feeling for tightened muscles that would indicate soreness. He laid his small pack on the ground beside the Winchester and began to rub down the horse with handfuls of dried grass.

When he was done he slipped on some handmade hobbles, turned the pony loose to feed, and went to rummage for his own evening meal.

There was nothing to do but to curl up in one of the blankets and take advantage of the time to sleep. The horse would not be able to travel farther until it had rested.

I made the wrong choice, he murmured to himself as he settled in the blanket. *I should have headed directly home. She has lengthened the distance between us now. I will need to be up at first light. If the pony isn't ready to travel, I will send him home. I cannot have him holding me back.*

❧   ❧   ❧

One day blurred into another. Running Fawn's bread and cheese were gone. Her feet were swollen and cut and bruised from sharp grasses and ragged stones. Still she stumbled on.

I must get home, was the constant refrain in her head. One that pushed Running Fawn forward, even though she was forcing one foot in front of the other with little awareness or direction. But a new thought was trying hard to surface. One that she had been fighting against. She was in trouble. Confused. She had lost her sense of bearing. Her ability to think rationally. At last, common sense prevailed. *I must rest and refresh myself or I will never make it*, she scolded gently.

For a moment she sat where she had dropped, her head whirling, her senses numbed. She had to think. Had to reason. She could not keep pushing forward, without food, without water. She pressed her hand to her forehead and willed the buzzing sensation to stop.

Water.

First I need water.

The river was off to her left. She knew that much. But she had no idea how far away it was or if she would be able to make it. *Wait*, a small voice inside seemed to dictate. *Wait until the day cools.*

She lifted her head and looked for shade. Off to her right was a small bush. She had to go there. Had to rest in the shade.

She dragged herself back on her painful feet and slowly moved to the small growth and fell in its shadow.

I will sleep, she told herself. *I will sleep until nightfall.*

She curled up in a ball, her blanket-dress pulled tightly around her, and allowed herself to drift off into a deep sleep.

❧   ❧   ❧

The little pony proved to have a stout body and willing heart, and though Silver Fox knew he had to rest the horse at night, it was always willing to go on with the first light of dawn. As he traveled, the young man's respect for the small animal grew. As he rubbed him down at the end of another sweltering day, he knew now that it would have been hard for him to turn the horse loose, hoping it would find its way home. He had become attached to the plucky little pony.

"You are a tough bronc, I'll hand that to you," he said as he slipped on the hobbles. He let his hand trail down the horse's neck, sending it off to graze with an affectionate pat.

As he turned from the animal, his thoughts turned to more troubling ones. He had been on the trail for four days, and he had found no sign of Running Fawn. By now her supplies would have run out. What was she doing for food? Was she still okay? What should he be doing that he wasn't?

He sat and pondered hard as he munched on his rations.

At long last he had made up his mind. He would backtrack. He must have passed her by. He would backtrack and then zigzag back and forth across the prairie. It would add many miles to the distance he must travel, but it seemed to be his only chance of finding her.

Chapter Thirteen

Travel

When Running Fawn awoke, the half moon was casting a weak light on the prairie landscape, giving the earth an eerie appearance. A soft wind blew away some of the heat. Running Fawn welcomed the coolness and drew her blanket garment closer about her body.

She felt prepared to think and plan now. She should have realized earlier the effect the intense heat had on her brain. She could have perished without even knowing that she was in trouble.

Now she sat calmly, fingering the pillowcase that lay before her on the ground. It contained nothing now—nothing but the length of cord and the pair of useless oxfords. She lifted the case and let the shoes tumble out on the ground. They really were only a burden to her. She reached down and lifted one, then dropped it again. Why should she carry something that was of no use?

Then she picked it up again, untied it, slipped the lace from the eyes and laid the shoe aside. She reached for the mate and repeated the process. Tying the two laces together she made a cord long enough to easily reach around her waist. It would help to have her blanket tied securely. Her hands would be freed for other tasks.

Do I keep this? she asked herself of the empty pillowcase. She certainly did not need it to carry the small bit of cord.

She could tie that about her body, too.

I will take it. It might come in handy. I wish it would hold water, she mused.

Running Fawn smiled at the thought of the white cotton holding water for her journey, then stuffed the cord back into the case and wrapped the whole thing about her shoulders.

Water was her first concern. She started off through the moonlight in the direction that would lead to the river.

I wonder how far away I have drifted? she asked herself.

But she had not traveled for long before she could smell the river on the night air. Her steps quickened. Once she had alleviated her thirst she would be free to consider other needs.

The water was cool as she lifted it to her lips and then splashed it over her face and arms. The wind cooled her body further as it evaporated the droplets. She sat with her swollen feet in the water and felt refreshed.

Now I must have food, she thought as she stood and looked around the riverbank in the moonlight.

She knew what her food supply must be. Prairie jackrabbits abounded. She would need to snare her meal.

It took a good deal of effort and the rest of the night, but at last she was successful. She had carefully set traps fashioned from her cord and branches, and she did not give up until she had snared two of the animals.

The moon had dipped behind a cloud and left her with little light. On hands and knees she began to grope around in search of a sharp stone that would aid her in skinning the animals.

She found one that would meet her need just as the moon reappeared in the distant west and the first rays of the sun began to lighten the sky in the east.

She felt good about her catch. The skins would make a protective covering for her feet, and the meat would sustain her on the trail. She would search for flint stones so she might build a fire to roast a portion. But if she failed, she would partake of the uncooked meat. It was better than starving. The rest of the meat she would cut into long strips and dry in the hot sun. Once pounded and cured, it would keep for days.

She did not try to travel but rested in the makeshift camp for the entire day. She had made a foolish error in judgment by traveling in the heat of the sun without taking care to have plenty of water. She would not repeat the same mistake.

Once her meat was prepared and stretched out to dry, and the skins were cleaned as thoroughly as she could with the sharp stone, she pulled the blanket closely about her body and lay in the coolness of the small bushes growing along the stream's edge.

⚜   ⚜   ⚜

Silver Fox backtracked for two days before he turned his mount and started his zigzag search of the prairie. It took him an additional three days to return to the farthest point he had been in his journey.

He was worried and discouraged as he prepared to camp for the night. Again he was tempted to free the pony and continue on foot.

"I think I have forgotten my tracking skills," he said to the animal as he rubbed him down. "Surely there should have been *something* for me to pick up on by now."

He had bent down to place the hobbles on the front feet of the horse when his eyes spotted something in the dim light of evening.

Carefully he lifted back the blades of grass and let his fingers trace out the small indentation. Yes. He was sure. It was the faint outline of a footprint.

Barefoot, he noted to himself. *She is not wearing the shoes. Feet bare—and swollen.*

On hands and knees he carefully crawled forward, searching out the next step. He found it. The left foot did not seem to be as badly bruised and swollen as the right.

Forward he went, step by step. The prints were not even nor in a straight line. She seemed to be staggering as she walked. She was in need of help, of that he was sure.

By her footprints, Silver Fox could tell she was not heading directly toward the camp but was off course. And she was moving away from the river rather than toward it. He raised himself to stare off into the gathering darkness. Then he returned to the pony.

"You are tired and hungry, I know," Silver Fox said to the little animal. "I cannot ask you to travel farther tonight. But in the morning—perhaps we will find her. Her trail is not more than a few days old."

Silver Fox felt many emotions as he settled down for the night. He was relieved to see some indication that she was still alive—at least as of a few days ago. He grieved at the suffering she must be enduring. He was impatient to be back on her trail, but he could not ask for more from the small pony. The animal was already near exhaustion.

It was an unusually long time before Silver Fox could quiet his whirling thoughts enough to drop off to sleep.

In the morning he ate quickly, not bothering to build a fire. Then he set off for the pony to begin the day's journey. He hoped he could hold his impatience in check and not push the animal too fast.

He had nearly reached the small horse when his eyes spotted an unusual object in the grass off to his left, and he went to take a look at it.

As he approached he could see that it was a shoe. His pace quickened. Yes. Yes, it was one of the oxfords. Left behind, minus the lace. She had been wise to take the lace. He let his gaze drift out further and then saw the second oxford almost buried in a stand of tall grass. Its lace also was missing.

He bent down to trace her footsteps. She was heading directly for the river now, and she did not seem to be staggering. She must have stopped to rest and sorted out her confusion.

She was still able to think. To reason.

Relieved, he quickly caught the pony and swung up on his back.

"Friend," he said to the horse, "we are getting close. Let's find her."

The pony responded to the urgency in his voice and started off at a trot.

❦ ❦ ❦

After a few days of rest while she allowed her bruised feet to heal, Running Fawn was ready to travel on. She gathered her remaining meat scraps from the bushes where she had hung them to dry and placed them in the pillowcase.

The meat would have been better with crushed berries, she thought to herself, but she knew that it would nourish her on the trail in spite of that lack.

She had also gathered some edible roots and leaves. They were not her favorite source of food, but they would add to her limited diet. *I much prefer mountain herbs*, she thought as she placed the items in the sack with the meat. *These are bitter*.

She had taken advantage of her resting time to make natural poultices for her feet. The herbal portions mixed with the river water had greatly eased the pain from her swollen feet and started the healing process. *If I just had a few more days*, she thought, *they would be almost whole again*.

But she did not have more time. She feared that she had taken too long already. Her father might have died in the time that she was delayed. Agitation spurred her to get back on her journey.

Carefully she wound up her cord. She would need it for trapping again. She judged that she was only about halfway home.

Her next task was to bind the skins, fur side in, around her feet. She used the laces from the shoes to tie them on, for she did not wish to cut the cord into shorter lengths.

It was getting toward twilight and the heat of the day was

beginning to lessen. She determined that she would now travel by night rather than by day. The hot sun and lack of water almost had left her senseless. She would not risk it again.

Now she would follow the river's path, even though the trail would be much longer. She knew that it would eventually lead her to the camp. She would not risk diverting from its banks.

Gathering her small bundle on her shoulder, she prepared to set off. She had taken only a few steps when she noticed a rider top the ridge to her right. A feeling of fear swept through her. She had been seen. She should have been more wary. Now that he knew she was there, there was no place to hide.

She started walking briskly, hoping the unknown rider would be intent on reaching the river and give her little notice. But the horse altered its course. The rider was obviously planning to cut her off.

She cast her eye across the river. Should she swim?

But it seemed of little use. The horse would quickly make its way across the stream.

Nervously she lifted her eyes to the approaching rider. He lifted a hand in salute.

She stared. There was something about the movement that caught her attention. It was not the wave of a white rider. Was it an Indian rider on the pony? Who? From what tribe? Would he be a friend—or foe? He did not appear to be wearing buckskins.

Running Fawn felt terror ripple up and down her spine. There was no place to flee, so she stopped, turned and faced the unknown.

As the rider drew near, her frown deepened. It *was* an Indian—in white man's clothing. Though she could not see him clearly through the gathering twilight, there was something strangely familiar about his carriage. He sat on the pony like—but no—that was impossible. Silver Fox was back at school.

Running Fawn let her white pillowcase slide slowly off her shoulder and rest on the ground at her feet. The pony had increased its speed and was covering the distance at a brisk trot.

"It *is*," she said in English with a little intake of air. "It is Silver Fox."

He slid to the ground while his mount was still in motion—then just stood there. Stood and stared, as though trying to read her condition all in a moment of time. At last he nodded.

"You are well?" he asked in their native tongue.

It was her turn to nod, mutely.

"That is good," he replied.

He took a step forward, one hand extended, but she knew he did not mean to shake her hand. Did not mean to touch her. She did not advance to meet him—just stood and stared, wanting to weep for some unexplained reason. Just before he reached her he stopped again. His eyes were still intently fixed on her face.

"We feared for your well-being," he said simply.

Running Fawn knew that the pronoun included those at the boarding school. Again terror gripped her heart. No. Not now. Not after all she had been through.

"They asked you . . . to take me back?" she asked simply.

"Yes," he answered.

With resignation her shoulders drooped. It was as she thought. She would never see her father again.

To him she said slowly, "Do you not understand? Have you forgotten our people?"

He shook his head, his dark eyes glistening in the light that still lingered.

"No," he said evenly. "No, I have not forgotten. I told them I would take you home."

❧　　❧　　❧

He convinced her to camp for the night. The pony was too

tired to move on. Now that they had joined forces the travel would be much faster. He had supplies, a canteen for water, he explained. They would not need to follow the river so closely but could take the route that would lead them directly to the Reserve, detouring only when they came to a farm site or a ranch.

She reluctantly agreed and laid aside her small bundle.

He built a fire and spread out the food he still carried. She looked long at the little supply and then asked him if she could make some bannock. He smiled. She quickly and expertly prepared the familiar staple.

"Let me see your feet," he ordered gently when they had finished their meal. She was reluctant, but obediently unwrapped the rabbit skin. In the glow from the fire, he carefully examined one foot and then the other. They were scarred and bruised with some unhealed abrasions, but there was no sign of infection.

"Put more of your healing salve on them and leave them open to the air overnight," he suggested, and she nodded and laid aside the skins.

"We will travel with first morning light," he continued. "It is best that you sleep now."

Running Fawn nodded assent and began to wrap her blanket garment more closely to her body.

He went to his pack and came back with two blankets that he handed to her. He would sit by the fire for most of the night, or rest on the open ground, he told her.

She started to protest but he stopped her. "You must be rested for the journey," he replied.

She took the blankets and spread one on the ground and wrapped the other snugly about her. She felt too full of thoughts and questions to sleep. Too full of conflicting emotions. There was so much she wished to know.

At last she spoke into the darkness.

"Are they angry?"

He stirred slightly and looked over at her.

"Angry? No. Worried. Very worried."

She thought about his words for many minutes, then she spoke again.

"I need to pay them—for the things I took," she confessed.

"Yes," he answered.

"Do you need to pay them?" she asked, remembering the supplies and the horse.

"No," he answered again. "They gave."

She was relieved about that. At least she had not caused him also to have a big debt.

She lay in silence for many more minutes.

"How did you find me?" she asked softly.

The question filled the darkness between them. *How did I find you?* he repeated the words silently in his heart. With her traveling one way over the vast prairie, and him on another course, how had he found her? If he had not bent down to tie the hobbles at that very spot where she had stepped—? And with her plans to travel by night and his to travel by day—? If he had not found her when he did, would he *ever* have found her? Would she have made it alone?

At last he spoke. His voice was soft in the stillness of the night.

"They pray," was all he said.

Chapter Fourteen

The Storm

They were up and on their journey before the morning sun was even showing on the horizon. Silver Fox decided that now that he had located Running Fawn he would change his pattern. They would travel through the early morning until the sun was reaching its peak in the sky, then rest during the heat of the afternoon while the pony grazed, and again take to the homeward trail in the cool of the long twilight.

Though she yearned to spend every possible moment on the trail, Running Fawn agreed to the plan. She knew she had pressed herself too hard those first days.

"You ride," insisted Silver Fox and gave Running Fawn a hand up onto the pony's back.

She did not argue. He already had much to say about the need for her feet to complete their healing.

As planned, they traveled until noon, then the pony was allowed to feed and rest while they tried to find shelter from the sun.

As soon as the heat began to lessen, Silver Fox whistled for the pony and they continued their journey, eating from Running Fawn's dried meat as they traveled.

By the time they stopped for the night the water canteen was empty, so Silver Fox decided to visit a farm building that lay off to their right. He would have walked but the pony needed watering too.

Running Fawn tried to sleep while she awaited his return, but she could not control her misgivings about his mission. What if he should not be welcomed? What if the farmer decided that the young Indian was a threat? Was he in danger?

She finally heard him approaching their campsite. She stood to watch him draw near.

"Have you water?" she called.

"Yes," he answered and lifted the canteen while she breathed a sigh of relief.

She stood silently until he entered the camp and lowered the canteen to her waiting hands. "They also filled this big bottle for me," he said, grinning and holding the bottle up for her to see. "It is two days' supply—or a drink for the pony, whichever is needed."

Running Fawn looked at the bulky bottle. Though it would be difficult to manage on the horse or in the blanketed sling that Silver Fox carried over his shoulder, it would make their journey much easier—and quicker.

"The man said there is a spring ahead, about two days' journey. We can fill again there. Then he advises that we follow the river. Up ahead, it turns and leads almost directly to the Reserve."

That was very welcome news to Running Fawn.

"They also sent you this," he went on, drawing a small bundle from the large one he held.

Running Fawn stared in disbelief at the familiar-looking buckskins he held up.

"They trade with the Sarcee," Silver Fox explained.

Running Fawn sighed as her initial amazement and relief turned to the fact that now she had even greater debt to repay.

"I traded two tins of oily fish," he said lightly. He smiled. "The farmer's wife said she is so tired of salt pork and venison steak that she could hardly swallow another bite, so she welcomed the tins of fish."

There would be no further burden of debt. The garments had been purchased, thanks to Silver Fox's bartering.

She could not wait to get into real clothes, and she clutched them to her as she hurried off to switch from her wrap-around blanket into the buckskins. There were even a pair of moccasins for her feet, and Running Fawn thanked the tins of fish that had provided her with such comfort. She felt that she had once again become a whole person. The Sarcee garments differed only slightly from those of the Blackfoot, and she was thankful to Silver Fox for thinking of her needs.

❧   ❧   ❧

After the two days, they had indeed run out of water. The pony had required a share of the bottled water since an unusually dry year had meant no streams or even a small slough. But they found the spring as the farmer had promised. With immense thankfulness they knelt at the water's edge and drank deeply along with the pony.

Then they rested. The long days of travel were taking their toll.

❧   ❧   ❧

"It is going to rain," observed Silver Fox the next morning.

Running Fawn lifted her eyes to the sky. All she saw was a wispy cloud far to the northwest.

"Thunderstorm by afternoon," Silver Fox predicted.

The small bit of white on the horizon looked so harmless, so scattered, that it was hard for her to believe it could carry enough power to be a thunderstorm by the afternoon, but she did not argue with Silver Fox. She did notice his stride lengthen as though he wished to cover as many miles as possible before the storm struck. The pony quickened his pace to keep step.

"What is his name?" Running Fawn asked after they had traveled some time in silence. Silver Fox turned to look at her.

"The horse," she explained. "What is his name?"

"I do not know."

"They did not name him?"

"I suppose they did. But Otis did not tell me—and I did not ask."

"You should name him," she mused after further silence.

He dropped back to walk beside the pony. "Name him if you wish," he offered.

Running Fawn sat up straighter and smiled in delight. She had never named an animal before. She wasn't sure if she should pick a name that would suit an Indian pony or a name like the horses from the boarding school stable.

Prancer? Yellow Mane? Prince? Quonto?

At length she spoke in English, "What do you think of Little Giant?"

He laughed softly at her choice and reached up to pat the neck of the sweating animal.

He answered her in the same language. "Little Giant? That is good. That suits him—just fine."

⚜   ⚜   ⚜

By midafternoon the clouds were rolling toward them, dark and menacing. The wind that accompanied them was blowing strong and held a chill. Silver Fox took Little Giant's reins to move him forward at a faster pace. But it was not long until the storm's full fury was upon them. Dark clouds, with a frightening white streak through the center, were bearing down upon them, and the strong wind pushed against their progress.

"Hail," Silver Fox shouted into the wind, then hail blew into their faces. "We should find cover."

Running Fawn looked around them. As far as the eye could see was open prairie. Not even a small shrub offered any kind of shelter from the storm.

"I think we should stop," Silver Fox reiterated, "and do what we can for protection before the hail strikes."

He offered a hand to Running Fawn and she slid down off the pony. She wondered what they could possibly do for protection from the storm.

"The blankets—" Silver Fox was saying as he slipped the bridle from the pony. "Get all the blankets from the pack."

"Blankets will not stop rain," argued Running Fawn.

"No, but they might be some shelter from the hail."

Quickly Running Fawn unrolled the bundle and pulled free the three blankets it contained.

"Fold them together."

Running Fawn obeyed.

"Now wrap them around you. Especially over your head," he ordered.

Running Fawn looked at him in concern.

"And you?" she asked simply.

"I will be fine," he answered just as large drops of cold rain began to beat down in earnest upon them.

Lightning flashed and thunder rumbled angrily across the darkening sky. The wind had reached gale proportions. Running Fawn was glad she was wearing the buckskins and had the added protection of the extra blankets.

"The pony," she cried, watching the small animal drift away, head down with the wind.

"We will have to see to him later," Silver Fox shouted against the noise of the storm and the first icy balls of hail pelting down with the rain. "Quickly," he yelled. "Get under cover."

Running Fawn sank to the ground and held the blankets up for him to join her.

"No," he shouted in response. "I will be fine. Wrap them around your head and shoulders."

Running Fawn rose to her feet and cast the blankets to the side on the ground.

"If you plan to face the storm," she called against the wind, "so will I."

He stared at her in frustration, then swept up the blankets, pushed her to a sitting position, and threw the blankets around their shoulders. Huddled together they felt the full assault of the storm as the hail began to pommel them.

For minutes that seemed like hours, wind-driven jagged balls of ice pounded them on the head, the back, the shoulders, while cold rain beat down on them and formed a puddle beneath them. By the time the hail had diminished, Running Fawn was shivering uncontrollably. Her garments were soaked through and her hair was dripping. The cold rain continued to fall, and the force of the wind seemed to drive the chill to her very bones.

Silver Fox finally lifted away the sodden blankets.

"Are you all right?" he asked her.

She managed to nod her head. She was too cold to speak.

"You have some welts," said Silver Fox, looking at her bare arms. Running Fawn was sure her back was just as bruised. Because he was wearing a long-sleeved shirt, she could not tell if Silver Fox had bruises on his arms.

"I . . . I think I am fine," she finally said through stiff lips. She noticed that she did not have to yell to be heard. The wind was dying down.

He nodded.

"Do you think the sun will return?"

Silver Fox stared at the sky. The rain was still falling and the clouds seemed to stretch all the way to the northern horizon.

"I think it will rain for some time," he answered.

Running Fawn shivered. It seemed that there would be no way to get dry. Even though they had matches, there would be no dry fire material, and a fire could not be kept burning with the rain pelting down.

"We may as well walk," said Silver Fox. "Are you able?"

Running Fawn nodded, then cast an anxious glance around.

"What about Little Giant?" she asked.

"He will have drifted with the storm. I'm afraid we cannot take time to look for him. It will be dark before long."

Running Fawn knew in her heart that he was right, but she hated to lose the pony. Besides the welcome relief for her feet, he had become a friend. Had he been able to endure the hail? One of the big stones on his head could be disastrous.

"Let's try to wring out the blankets."

She took one end and together they tried to twist them free of their sodden load. Water ran on the ground, but the coarse wool had soaked up the rain like a sponge, and the blankets still were much heavier than they should have been. They bundled their provisions into soggy piles. Without a pony to share the load, Silver Fox laid aside the heavy bottle, now empty and too cumbersome to tote along. The young man lifted the smaller bundle to Running Fawn's shoulder, then hoisted his own, including the rifle.

Together they trudged on through the somewhat gentler storm.

🌿   🌿   🌿

They pushed on until it was too dark to see. The rain had ceased to fall, but they were very wet. With night coming and the cold wind still blowing against them, they were both shivering uncontrollably in spite of their exertion.

"We must stop," said Silver Fox.

Running Fawn was only too glad to quit for the night. Her whole body ached from struggling through the mud, carrying her load. But to stop walking meant they would no longer have the little bit of warmth generated from their movement.

"It will be cold," noted Silver Fox. "Everything is wet."

Running Fawn nodded, her teeth chattering.

"The blankets will be of no use."

She knew that.

"We cannot build a fire."

She knew that too.

"It will not be a pleasant night."

He was right, but she was too cold to comment.

"Let me see if I can pile the bundles to break the wind a little," said Running Fawn, and he worked in the dark to make some kind of wind shelter, using the rifle to prop up one edge.

"That is the best that I can do," he said finally.

It wasn't much, but it did help. Running Fawn sat down on the sodden ground behind the blankets and pulled her knees up tight against her chest. It was now so dark she only felt Silver Fox lower himself to the ground at her side. At first she held herself apart, self-conscious and shivering.

She had not forgotten that she did not share his ideas. He had always been more open in accepting the ways of the white man than she felt he should be. They still had not resolved those differences, though on the trail they had made an unspoken agreement to lay them aside for the time being. She was so thankful that he had come to help her find her way home that she was glad to accept his help, regardless of his interest in learning the white man's ways. In the days they had traveled together, she simply would not let herself think about their difference of opinion.

Now as they sat shoulder to shoulder in the darkness of the stormy night, she dared to think that perhaps he had changed. She wanted him to change. She wanted him to care as much for their people, for their history, their ways, as she herself did.

There was something about him—a depth to his character—that drew her to him in spite of her resolve to hold herself aloof. He was someone she admired. Someone with great strength. If only he would forsake his fascination with this new learning and return to the ways of his past. The old ways had served their fathers. They were good enough. If only . . .

But wait. He had left the boarding school. He had voluntarily taken to the trail. Didn't that mean—? He was taking her home—back to the Reserve. Surely it must mean . . . He was going back too. He was going home to their people.

In the cold darkness she leaned just a little more toward him.

Chapter Fifteen

Reunion

Running Fawn struggled to her feet in the morning and found herself to be so stiff that she had a hard time moving.

Silver Fox was already walking about, flexing his own stiff muscles, working his arms and legs. He smiled at her. "Did you know you had so many parts that could ache?" he asked her.

Running Fawn shook her head. Even that motion hurt. She reached up to feel a couple of sore spots that must have been from the pounding hail.

There were blue bruises on her arms, and she knew from the way her back and shoulders felt that she was bruised there as well.

"Walk around a bit—slowly," advised Silver Fox, "then we will begin our journey."

Running Fawn obeyed.

As soon as they were reasonably free of their cramped muscles, they started out. With no pony for Running Fawn to ride, she tried to keep stride with Silver Fox. But she noticed several times he had to consciously slow his pace to match hers.

Silver Fox observed, "We should have no problem with a water supply," and Running Fawn nodded. The heavy rain of the day before had filled low-lying slough bottoms. It also made walking more difficult.

They walked steadily on, their conversation only occasional. Running Fawn's moccasins felt twice their normal weight.

Soon the sun was shining brightly down upon them, sending dancing heat waves reflecting off the sodden ground. The whole world steamed. The day promised to be another scorching one. Running Fawn felt the chill leaving her body. She knew it would not be long until she would be longing for just a bit of the coolness of the night.

They stopped to rest around noon and ate from their diminishing food supply and drank from the common canteen.

Running Fawn was beginning to feel drowsy with the heat and the lack of real sleep. Silver Fox seemed to notice.

"Perhaps we should stay here during the heat of the day and walk when it begins to cool off."

Running Fawn nodded, in spite of her inner urgency to keep on the move.

"It will give the blankets time to dry," went on Silver Fox and rose to unbundle the packs and spread the still-wet blankets out in the sun. At once they began to send little shivering breaths of steam upward.

Running Fawn found a smooth rock and curled up with her head resting on her arm. In just a few moments she was sound asleep.

When she awakened she noticed that Silver Fox had already wrapped up the two bundles. He appeared anxious to be on the trail, and she wondered why he had not awakened her. Now he looked at her, smiled slightly, and asked, "Do you feel better?"

Running Fawn nodded. She felt much better after her long rest.

"I do not think we are far from the river," he observed. "We can rest on its banks tonight."

Running Fawn lifted her pack. It was much lighter now that the blankets were dry.

She was ready to go. If they were near the river, then they would soon be home.

As they approached the river she noticed Silver Fox hesitate midstride. His head came up as his eyes swept the slope before them. Fear immediately sent a shivering signal down the length of Running Fawn's spine as she too paused to search the landscape.

But it was a deer, foraging on the river's green grasses.

"No," was Running Fawn's whispered plea as Silver Fox lifted the rifle to his shoulder.

The gun lowered, and Running Fawn felt her cheeks warm as the deer bounded to the safety of a hidden ravine.

She wondered if she should apologize. She knew Silver Fox's automatic response came from a tradition as old as time. But the deer had been such a beautiful, graceful sight as it lifted its head and stared at them with solemn, wide eyes.

She was about to open her mouth to speak when Silver Fox turned to her.

"We have no way to carry the meat," he said softly, as though it had been reason rather than emotion that had sabotaged the hunt. "One should never be guilty of waste."

Running Fawn nodded silently, inwardly thankful once again that she had not been born male. The role of hunter would be a difficult one. She did not envy Silver Fox his Winchester.

But as she walked, she smiled softly to herself. She had the strange feeling that Silver Fox was not sorry to have a valid excuse for allowing the beautiful animal to bound away unharmed.

❦   ❦   ❦

By the next evening they were close enough to the Reserve to see campfires and tents in the distance, though not those of their own band. Running Fawn felt her spirit lift and her body gain new energy. Soon . . . soon they would be home with their own people. Soon life would return to normal. She found it hard to be patient at their walking pace as they pressed on through the twilight.

❧   ❧   ❧

A small girl on the way to the river for water was the first one to notice the two travelers approaching. She turned and called and soon a woman poked her head out from a tent flap. Running Fawn heard the excited call but was too far away to understand the words.

More women and girls joined the little cluster and looked and pointed and talked excitedly.

Silver Fox raised an arm in greeting and the noise in the camp increased. Children broke loose and came running to meet them. Mothers called after them but it was encouragement, not concern, in their voices.

When they were near enough to hear the words, "Welcome, welcome," Running Fawn felt her heart quicken and her throat grow tight with emotion.

Soon they were surrounded by the chattering children asking questions and expressing welcome, all in noisy clamor.

"Where did you come from?" "How is your health?" "Welcome." "Have you had food?" "What is in your packs?" "Welcome." "Welcome." "Do you bring gifts?" "Welcome." "Welcome." "Welcome." Silver Fox laughed at the friendly confusion. Running Fawn wanted to bend down and hug each one of the youngsters.

She noticed inquiring glances her way and strange looks on some of the small faces and then remembered that she was wearing buckskins of the Sarcee.

"See," she explained, pointing to herself. "I have the Sarcee dress—but I am Blackfoot. Blackfoot—like you." Doubt still showed in some of the eyes.

The women approached more slowly than the children with a more decorous welcome. They, too, noticed Running Fawn's dress, and she felt compelled to explain again. She recognized none of the people.

They were welcomed to a campfire and given food. A few men had gathered and squatted around or sat on robes or blankets, anticipating any news of the world beyond their borders.

Silver Fox opened their bundles and handed the few items as gifts to their hosts. A blanket to the man, the knife and a small sack of beans to his wife. The canteen to the young son, who beamed with great pleasure. When he passed out the pony's bridle, Running Fawn wished to protest but she held her tongue. The remainder of the rabbit jerky was given to the children. They shared the treat, chewing off a bite before passing it on to the one next in line.

Silver Fox spoke then, explaining the reason for their long journey and their desire to get home quickly to see Running Fawn's father who was ill.

Dark eyes darkened further.

"There is much sickness. Much sickness," they said. "Many die."

Then one younger brave turned to Running Fawn. "Who is your father?" he asked her.

"Gray Hawk of Calls Through The Night's band," she replied.

He thought deeply for a moment, then nodded. "I know. They are on the other side of the Reserve," he noted.

Running Fawn felt her heart sink. She was home—yet she was not. The Reserve covered four hundred and seventy square miles. If her father was somewhere on the other side, they still had a long way to travel.

The man reached down and with his finger drew a map in the dust at his feet. Silver Fox moved closer and crouched on the ground, his eyes intent on the drawing. Running Fawn, still not recovered from her deep disappointment, was struggling with the thought of further travel.

It turned out that it was not as bad as it could have been. When Silver Fox turned back to her he held up a finger. "A long day's journey," he said and seemed pleased with the fact.

Running Fawn tried to look pleased too, but she felt only tired.

✢   ✢   ✢

That night they shared the tepee of one of the families and left early the next morning before the sun was up. Following the river seemed to be an almost direct route to the camp of their band, and so they traveled along its general course, keeping a listening ear for the gentle flow of the water.

Midafternoon they decided to draw closer to the stream for some rest from the sun and a refreshing drink from the flowing waters.

Silver Fox had just lowered the bundle with their few remaining supplies to the ground and stood to stretch his muscles when Running Fawn gave a little gasp.

Silver Fox jerked upright and turned to look in the direction her finger was pointing. There stood the pony, head up, ears perked forward, riverbank grasses hanging from the corners of his mouth.

"Amazing," said Silver Fox in English and started toward the small animal, Running Fawn close behind.

The pony did not seem to be harmed by the storm. Silver Fox ran his hands over his back, his neck, his head, and on over his withers and down his legs. The horse flinched on a few occasions but only as he might have done to dislodge a pestering fly.

"He has a few lumps," observed Silver Fox, "but nothing serious."

"Little Giant," murmured Running Fawn, passing a hand over his stout neck and ending with an affectionate pat, "we thought we would never see you again."

She turned to Silver Fox. "We have no bridle."

"You have the cord," he reminded her, nodding toward the bundle. They moved toward the small pack, Silver Fox leading the pony by a handful of his mane.

"Do you still wish to rest or should we go on?" asked Silver Fox after the cord had been fashioned into a bridle over the pony's head and around his nose.

Running Fawn knew he intended that she would ride again. The sun was very hot overhead, and she realized that Silver Fox too must be warm and weary. As much as she ached to be back on the trail and that much closer to home, she nodded toward the nearby cluster of stunted willow and said, "Let's rest a bit."

He nodded and handed her a blanket from the bundle and laid the other aside for himself.

Then he made a hobble of sorts from the pillowcase that had not been discarded. It was no longer a snowy white, having been used in many ways along the dusty trail. Running Fawn knew she would not be able to return it but would need to replace it. The ladies at the boarding school would not be wanting such a stained and torn item back.

The hobble would not have been needed. When Running Fawn opened her eyes later, the pony lay on the grass a short distance from the two forms on their blankets. He seemed as pleased to see them as they had been to see him.

Soon on their way again, they passed tents or simple houses and exchanged greetings with their occupants. Running Fawn found it hard to not linger for a chat, even though she was impatient to be on her way. It was so nice to be hearing her own familiar language.

They did not make it to their own group that evening but joined another family for the night, shared the meal from the cooking pot, and visited around the fire.

Running Fawn was welcomed into the crowded tent, but Silver Fox declined and slept in the open. There was little room in the tent for extra bodies.

Early the next morning Running Fawn arose, stepped carefully over sleeping forms, and joined Silver Fox. Her heart beat rapidly. By the time the sun was casting a full shadow, she would be with her family, her father.

Running Fawn was sure she could never stand the tension of this final leg of their journey as the prairie miles slipped slowly beneath their feet. Silver Fox seemed to sense her agitation.

Even Little Giant picked up on their mood and his steps quickened. As the morning advanced, Running Fawn noticed that the steps of Silver Fox were beginning to lag. The long days of travel and the heat of the sun had taken their toll. She was glad there was now no bundle to carry. They had given the last of their supplies to the family from the previous night. But she felt guilty that her impatience was pushing the young man beyond his strength.

"Why do you not ride?" she asked quietly.

He shook his head.

She waited some time before she spoke again.

"Little Giant is rested. He would carry two."

Silver Fox stopped and his eyes traveled over the pony. His sides were wet from the heat of the sun but he did not look overly tired.

"Perhaps," he responded.

Running Fawn slipped quickly from the animal's back, wanting to get his agreement while he was open to the idea.

Silver Fox accepted the cord rein and drew himself up onto the pony's back. Then he reached down a hand for Running Fawn. Taking his hand and stepping up on his positioned foot, she was given a boost to the animal's back behind him.

The pony tossed his head and set off, his hooves beating a steady rhythm on the prairie sod.

It was midmorning when they approached a group of familiar tents belonging to their own band. One With The Wind was the first to look up from stirring the cooking pot and see the small horse with its two riders. She called and soon others were milling about, pointing and talking to each other as they waited to identify the visitors.

The two were almost to the little group before Silver Fox was recognized and the idle chatter became excited calls. Running Fawn could wait no more. As Little Giant moved forward, she slipped from the back of their mount. She stood silently, looking at her people.

Tears pressed against her eyelids, but she blinked them back. She would not weep. Not now. She was home. Home. The word held magic.

Her eyes quickly scanned the gathering group. There was old toothless Bitter Woman. Running Fawn was surprised that she had escaped all the sickness. And there was Scar Nose—and Single Tooth and, yes, little Mountain Dove. How she had grown. And then, there before a fire, stood her friend, Laughing Loon. She had grown into a lovely maiden now. A maiden with dark, shy eyes and a gently curved body that even loosely flowing buckskins could not hide.

Running Fawn found it hard not to run. Not to call. Not to go racing into the camp to embrace each member of her tribal family. But she stood, silent and dignified, waiting for Silver Fox to dismount and lead the way. She was back to her own people. She was back to her own ways.

Chapter Sixteen

The Unexpected

Running Fawn felt her stomach tighten as they neared the tepee of her father. He had moved since she had been home—but that was not uncommon.

"Does Gray Hawk still live?" Silver Fox had asked the little cluster of excited people.

"He lives," had come the reply.

"His son, Crooked Moose?"

"He hunts."

"Where is Gray Hawk's lodging?"

A long, thin finger pointed. "Over the small hill, on the path to the river."

So they had crossed over the hill and found the path that led to the river. A lone tent stood in a circle of bare ground. In front, a cooking fire had burned out. There was no wisp of blue-gray, curling gently upward into the motionless air. A blackened kettle hung on the tripod, but no steam rose from the contents. Two deer hides, draped over a stick frame, were set to dry in the sun. Running Fawn could see at a glance that they were past the prime time for curing.

Silver Fox brought the pony to a halt, but Running Fawn did not move to dismount. She could not have explained her hesitation after the long, long anxious days on the trail, except that a fear gripped her very being, making her reluctant to face what might lie behind those tent flaps.

158

At least he lives, she reminded herself. *He lives. I have come in time.*

Silver Fox reached out a hand to help her down and slowly she swung off the horse's back.

Still she hesitated. He seemed to understand.

"I will go," he said softly and handed Running Fawn the rein before she could protest.

Already night's blackness was closing in upon them. It would be dark in the tent. She knew that no warm fire would glow to give light. It was too warm for inside fires, and besides, her father had no one to tend it for him.

Running Fawn felt herself stiff with tension as she waited for Silver Fox to reappear. What had he found? Was her father even now leaving to join the Great Spirit? Had she been too late after all?

The flap on the tent fluttered, then lifted and Silver Fox slipped out. Running Fawn could see a faint glow outlining his form. There was some kind of light in the dark tent after all.

"I have lit the lamp," he explained.

"Lamp?" queried Running Fawn.

"Lantern—of the white man."

"Where—?"

"They trade now," Silver Fox commented. "Much has changed."

Running Fawn said nothing. She did not need to be reminded.

"He waits for you." Silver Fox nodded toward the tent.

"Is he—" she began but couldn't finish the question.

She could see the shine of his eyes, the slight indication of a smile in the gathering darkness.

"You will see," he encouraged.

She turned to enter, her heart still thumping in her chest. Just before she ducked into the tepee she turned once again.

"And you?" she asked softly.

"I go to my father," he answered.

She held his gaze with hers in the stillness. There was so

much she wanted to say. Yet she did not know how to say it. Even the white man's English, with its many words, failed to express what she was feeling.

At last she whispered just two words. Two words that she hoped he would understand. Two words that came in English, though she could not have explained why.

"Thank you."

She dipped her head, lifted the flap, and entered the tent.

℞ ℞ ℞

He lay on a heap of buffalo robes in the corner, coarse blankets covering his shrunken frame. He did not stir, and she wondered for one frightening moment if he was no longer able to move.

She dropped to her knees and crawled forward over the skins on the floor. With one hand she reached out to him, touching the creased cheeks with trembling fingers.

"You have come," she heard his quivering voice whisper.

She was weeping then. Full, salty droplets that squeezed from under her eyelids and washed down her sun-browned face.

"I have come," she repeated.

"It is good." A deep sigh escaped him, making his whole frail body tremble.

She stroked his cheek and gently brushed aside the graying hair that wisped about his weathered face.

There was so much she wanted to know, needed to ask— but it would wait. There was no need to talk now. She was home. He was still alive. That was all that mattered.

℞ ℞ ℞

She was up before the sun, building the fire and putting on the cooking pot. It was as she had feared. The blackened kettle held only water. Crooked Moose had not returned. She would need to find something for them to eat. Her father needed meat for nourishment. She wanted to have something ready for him by the time he awoke.

There was a small garden to the left, but the few scraggly plants looked to have been left unattended and were withered and dried from summer's sun. She knew the garden needed water, and carrying water from the nearby river to care for the plants was woman's work. Crooked Moose would not favor taking on the task. He would be much more at ease with hunting game for the cooking pot.

But she could not wait for Crooked Moose to return. Her father needed food. She set out to see what she could find.

Two small boys fished along the riverbank. One already had three fish lying at his feet. She longed to strike a bargain but could think of nothing that she had to barter. She passed them by.

She thought of her bit of cord and wished she had it with her. She might be able to snare a jackrabbit. But she reminded herself that it was now sunup. The rabbits would be hiding out for the daylight hours and would not come out to feed again until twilight.

There seemed nothing to do but to find some prairie plants for a simple stew. They would not be much nourishment, but at least it would provide something to tide them over until she had a chance to meet with the Indian Agent and request a few needed supplies.

The first rays of sun already carried warmth and promised another day of intense heat. She was adding fuel to the fire for the stew when she heard the sound of horse's hooves.

Expecting to see Crooked Moose returning from the hunt, she lifted herself slightly and found the short prayer of her people raising in her throat, though not spoken aloud. *May the Sun God have smiled upon him. May he bring meat for the cooking pot. Nourishment for all who live within our tepee.*

But it was not Crooked Moose who pulled his horse to a stop near the campsite. Silver Fox swung down lightly and turned to silently hand her a bundle wrapped in deer hide.

Running Fawn recognized the way it was bundled, the way it was presented. It was meat. Sustenance. Nourishment.

Confusion washed over her face. Was Silver Fox being Indian? Or white? Was there significance in the extended hands? Or was it simply an offer of good will that he had learned at the boarding school?

She did not know. Could not ask.

A young brave brought meat as a gift. As more than a gift. As an indication that he was willing to provide for a maiden for the rest of her lifetime. That he was a worthy suitor, a good provider, a man intent upon taking on the role of her husband.

And if the maiden accepted his gift, she was giving her answer. It was not misunderstood.

Their eyes met—and locked. Running Fawn tried to read the message that his held. But she could not understand—fully. She had been too long away from her own people. He had been away too long. Did they still use the language of their people, both spoken and silent? She did not know. Felt unsure. Perhaps she was reading far more into the action than was intended.

She lowered her eyes and dipped her head in a slight nod. With a trembling hand she reached to receive the gift. She felt unsettled, confused—even as she felt a tremor of excitement pass through her. Was the chief's son actually proposing marriage? She still did not know. Her world was so different now. She no longer knew if the old ways still held. She would need to let the future answer for itself.

❧   ❧   ❧

By the time her father awoke, Running Fawn had calmed her troubled mind and had his savory meal of venison prepared and ready to serve.

He smiled as she knelt at his side and offered him the steaming broth. She was glad to see that his eyes were still bright, his voice steady, in spite of his having lost much weight.

"You are here," were his words of greeting.

She nodded and smiled.

"I feared I was only dreaming," he continued.

"No," said Running Fawn. "No, I am back. I will care for you now."

He was silent until she had finished feeding him. He sighed in contentment as the last spoonful was swallowed.

"Crooked Moose had a good hunt," he said, nodding in appreciation.

"Crooked Moose is not back," she informed him.

He frowned. "*You* hunted for venison?"

Running Fawn found herself smiling softly, both in amusement at his words and at the secret she carried. "No. No, Silver Fox shared his hunt," she finally brought herself to say.

"Silver Fox?"

Running Fawn nodded.

"Chief's son?"

She nodded again.

The old eyes began to glisten. It was clear to Running Fawn that her father was thinking of the old ways. He saw the gift of meat as far more than the willingness of a neighbor to share. "That is good," he said with a contented sigh.

Running Fawn wondered if she should remind her father that Silver Fox had lived away from the reservation for some time and might not intend to propose a future union. But she could not bring herself to speak the words. Her father would not understand how it had been at the school. How different the two worlds were. She held her tongue and said nothing.

᭟   ᭟   ᭟

After a morning rest, Gray Hawk announced that he wanted to be up to sit by the fire.

"The sun is warm," explained Running Fawn. "I have let the fire die."

He nodded. "I will sit by the fire ring," he insisted.

Running Fawn helped him up and placed a blanket over his frail shoulders. With her help he was able to leave the tepee and take a place on the ground in front of the fire's ashes.

"I will build the fire," she began, but he stopped her with a feeble wave of his hand.

"The sun is good," he said, and she knew that he did not need the fire.

She had started work on one of the drying hides. It would have been so much easier had it been done at the proper time, but she would do the best she could. The tanned hide would be needed.

She also had cut the remaining venison into long, thin strips and hung them in the hot sun to dry. Flies buzzed about the meat and she found herself continually swatting them away with a buffalo tail.

At last she turned to her father. He had been watching her silently.

"The flies are bad," she observed. "So many."

"Always many," he answered.

She wondered if there had always been such a plague of flies or if the number had increased. Had she just forgotten? Or had she simply paid no attention to them before?

She continued with her tanning.

Her father broke the silence. "They were good to you?" he asked, not needing to explain who he meant.

"They were good," she answered honestly.

He seemed pleased with her answer.

"You learned many things?" he asked after a few more moments of silence.

"Many things," agreed Running Fawn.

He pondered for some time before asking, "Do you believe their God?"

Running Fawn whirled around to face him, her eyes wide,

the shock showing on her face.

"No," she said hurriedly. "I kept my own—our own gods."

She wondered if she should say more. What had he thought? That she would betray her own people? Her own heritage?

But he did not appear to be condemning, though she could tell he was deep in thought. "Why?" he finally asked, his tone gentle.

Running Fawn was stunned. What was he asking? What did he want her to say? Was he really expecting an answer?

"I am . . . one of the people," she said, feeling somewhat bewildered and flustered. "We have always believed—"

He was shaking his head. "Things change," he said matter-of-factly. "Maybe the old gods went with the buffalo—no longer hear our prayers."

Running Fawn stared in disbelief. Then she spoke with vehemence. "They will come back. They will come back when we have found our way again."

"No," said the old man, shaking his head wistfully. "No, I do not think so. Perhaps they were all a dream. A vapor. Now they have vanished—like the sun when night comes."

"And like the sun they will return in the morning," argued Running Fawn, conviction in her voice.

"No." His one word was curt, final. Running Fawn wondered if she should go to him, comfort him.

But he did not seem despondent. He lifted his proud head and there was still determination in the dark eyes. "I have thought much," he said. "The God of Man With The Book speaks well. I believe He is the only God with real power. He must now be the God for our people."

Running Fawn could only stare.

Crooked Moose returned from the hunt, and across the front of his mount was the fresh carcass of an antelope.

After exchanging greetings, Running Fawn set to work to

preserve the meat. Her father was still beaming with the good news of the hunt when she turned to him.

"I prayed the Blackfoot prayer of the hunt," she informed him, hoping her words would also say that the old religion of the people still worked just fine.

His seamed face broke into a smile.

"I prayed also," he told her.

Now it was Running Fawn's turn to smile.

"See," she said. "We do still have a god."

"Yes," he confessed. "We do. I prayed to the God of heaven, in the name of Jesus His Son."

Running Fawn felt anger join her confusion. To return to a father who had laid aside the old religion for the God of the mission boarding school was something she never would have dreamed.

Her head lifted in defiance, something she had never done before. "Then I suppose we do not know which one answered," she said meaningfully.

He only smiled in reply.

Running Fawn could not imagine what had happened to her father.

Chapter Seventeen

Care

As Running Fawn knelt over the cooking fire, adding buffalo chips to the flame and stirring the pot, she was reminded that life for her people was not easy. She had a fleeting moment of longing for the large enameled stove of the mission school, with its even heat and easy accessibility to fuel.

She may have disliked those days bent over a hot iron pressing items that seemed a complete waste of her time, but she had to admit that the hand-turned washing machine was much easier than hoisting her laundry bundle and heading to the river.

If she had been totally honest or allowed herself the pleasure of any further reflection, she even might have admitted to missing a few of the mission's tasty dishes. But Running Fawn determined to close her mind to the past two years of her life and look steadfastly forward. She was Blackfoot. She was where she belonged, living the life to which she was born. If there were parts of it now that did not please her, she buried them deeply within and did not allow herself to think about them.

"Go see Man With The Book."
Gray Hawk spoke the words while Running Fawn leaned

over the fire, stirring the pot of seasoned stew. Even though the day had just begun she already felt tired. Her arms and back ached from the unaccustomed long hours of labor that had taken her time the previous day. The sun had set before she had the antelope meat on the drying racks and the hide scraped in preparation for tanning. She longed for a less busy and tiring day, even though she knew her work had really just begun.

She looked at her father with questioning eyes. Why was he commanding her to go see the white missionary? Surely he didn't expect her to learn more of his religion. She had been at the boarding school for two years listening to the talk about the Great God and His Son Jesus. If that had not convinced her, then it wasn't likely that anything else would.

"He needs food," went on her father in explanation. "He is ill."

"Does he not have someone to care for him?" asked Running Fawn.

"There is no one near him any longer. Old War Woman used to take him food. She is gone now. No one else lives close."

Running Fawn had noticed the distance between the tents. It seemed strange that they were now scattered over the prairies instead of forming a loose circle where they could enjoy one another's fires and companionship.

She straightened and looked at her father.

"Why?" she asked. "Why are the tepees so distant? Do my people no longer get along?"

He stirred and pulled his blanket closer about his shoulders. "It was the sickness," he answered. "The Agent thought the sickness would not spread from tent to tent if the people lived farther apart."

"But it didn't work, did it?" Running Fawn commented with a hint of bitterness. Ever since her return she had been hearing names of those who had not survived.

"They tried," said her father, resignation in his voice. "They did not have enough medicine for everyone."

168

"Perhaps they should have used the medicine of our people," retorted Running Fawn.

He shook his head. "The old medicine is not good for the new sickness," he responded.

His words only made Running Fawn more agitated. The new sicknesses would not have come if the white man had not brought them from their distant lands.

"Go see Man With The Book," he repeated now. "Take him some food from the pot."

Running Fawn knew she must obey but she hated the thought of a long trek across the prairie to visit someone she had no interest in. She placed another stick on the fire under the pot and turned to her father.

"You will be all right?"

He nodded. "Crooked Moose will be home soon."

Running Fawn was not so sure. She had seen little of her brother since she had been home. He slept late and then left as soon as he had filled his stomach with the food she had prepared, not giving any indication as to where he was going or how long he would be away.

"Do you want to go to your bed?" asked Running Fawn.

"I will sit in the sun," he responded. "I feel stronger now."

Running Fawn studied him carefully. He did look stronger, but surely just a few meals of nourishing food could not have made that much difference.

"You go," he prompted. "Make the journey before the sun is high."

Reluctantly she nodded.

"Where does he live?" she asked.

Her father picked up a small twig and drew a map on the ground. Running Fawn had no difficulty following the simple directions.

She placed some food in a small pail and set off, anxious to get the mission behind her.

But it turned out to be farther than she expected. By the time she reached the small crude dwelling, the sun was high in the sky and her face was flushed. She dreaded the long trip back home in the heat. Then she had to face the work of putting the hides to soak in the acid compound.

She wasn't sure how she should make her entry. Call and walk in as was the way of her people, or stop and knock on the door, waiting for an invitation, as the whites would do?

She decided to knock. The missionary was a white man—even though he had taken on many of the ways of her people.

There was no answer to her rap so she tried again. Still no response.

She didn't feel she should just turn around and go home. And she didn't want to leave the food on his doorstep. It would spoil quickly in the intense heat.

With hesitation she lifted the latch and pushed on the wooden door. It opened with a creak and she stepped inside.

For a moment she saw nothing as her eyes adjusted to the sudden change to darkness, and then she began to make out objects. A table. Stove. Chairs. Some garments hung on pegs. And a bed, up against the far wall.

At first she thought that it was empty, but then she realized that a form lay under the heap of blankets. She moved closer, hardly daring to breathe.

She scarcely recognized the missionary. His face was bearded and gaunt, his eyes shut. For one terrifying instance she thought that he was dead, and then she saw his eyelids flutter—ever so slightly.

She gathered her courage and moved closer. She could see that he was breathing shallowly.

"Reverend Forbes," she prompted, choosing to use his English name rather than the Indian one. "Reverend Forbes."

His eyes opened. He appeared to swallow. He did not answer.

She would not trouble him with further words. There was no need to ask if he was well. It was quite evident that he was not.

She set her small pail on the table and picked up an empty bucket that should have held water. As she hurried out, she wondered how long he had been without a drink.

There was a cistern in his yard. She hoped it was not dry and that the rope was available as she hurried toward it and pulled back the heavy lid. The rope was there and there was some water in the bottom, but there was an offensive odor that she could not identify. She knew they had been told they were not to use the river water, but surely the water from the stream was safer than this stagnant water from a nearly empty concrete container. She did not even bother replacing the cover, but grabbed up the pail and ran toward the river just over the hill.

When she returned he appeared to be in a deep sleep. She had to shake his shoulder to get his eyes to flutter open again. When she held the cup to his lips, more ran down his chin and dripped on the bedding than actually was swallowed.

But she did manage to get him to drink a few drops. It seemed to bring him closer to awareness.

She lowered his head and went for the stew. She would only be able to feed him the broth. He would never be able to chew. She would not stop to build a fire and heat the meal. He needed nourishment quickly. Besides, he was already flushed with fever.

She worked steadily to spoon the liquid into his mouth. Sometimes he managed to swallow, but more often the broth dribbled away.

Medicine. What he needs is medicine. Surely there must be medicine somewhere. Running Fawn looked around the room but saw nothing that looked like a medicine bottle.

She thought of the mission. Did they know how ill he was? Did they even *know* he was ill? Would they send someone to nurse him if they knew? Would they transport him to the city where he could be cared for properly?

What about the Agent? Did he know? Surely he would send some kind of help for another white man.

And the converts? The people who were supposedly attending his Bible classes in the newly constructed wood-frame church? What of them? Didn't any of them care?

Running Fawn puzzled over the whole affair as she tried to get some of the life-giving broth into his mouth.

Something had to be done or he would die. Maybe it was already too late to save him. But she had to try. Had to get him help someway. Even if she did not believe in his Gospel, she did have a measure of respect for the man. Had he not stood by the people when they were near starving? Had he not hunted and fished and nursed and fought for medicines? Certainly they owed him no less.

Running Fawn did what she could to make him comfortable and then left hurriedly. She had to get someone to help or he would be lost for sure.

❧   ❧   ❧

Crooked Moose was sitting in the shade of the tepee when she hurried back. Her father had retired to the coolness of the tent for an afternoon rest. Crooked Moose shaded his eyes against the harshness of the sun.

"Where have you been, in the heat of the sun?" he asked with some interest.

Running Fawn, hot and sweaty, did not even slow her stride till she stopped in front of him.

"We need to get help," she said hastily.

"Help?"

"For Man With The Book," she replied. "He is sick. Needs help. Medicine. We must get word to the Agent."

If she expected his immediate response, she was to be disappointed.

"He is always sick," he replied with little concern.

She stared at him. "He is *very* sick."

He shrugged careless shoulders.

She could not understand his attitude. "We need medicine," she said again, as though he had not understood. "From the Agent."

"The Agent does not have medicine," replied Crooked Moose. "It is all gone."

"Then they must get more."

Crooked Moose laughed. It was plain to Running Fawn that he thought she knew little about life on the Reserve.

"I will write to the mission," she said quickly. "They will send some."

He shifted his position on the ground and studied her, a look that bordered on cynicism curling back his lip.

"Many have died," he said carelessly. "Maybe one more."

His words angered Running Fawn. "Will you take a message to the Agent?" she asked directly.

For one moment he just looked up at her from where he lay on the ground, then he rolled over on his stomach and lowered his head to his arms. "No," he said emphatically. "He has a god. Let him pray."

Running Fawn had never heard such callousness, such bitterness from her brother. What had happened to him?

❧   ❧   ❧

She talked with her father.

"Why has no one helped Man With The Book?"

"They have. Many times."

"You mean, he has been sick before?"

"As many times as the geese go south."

"What is his sickness?"

"I do not know."

"Why did they not help him this time?"

"Neighbors are too far away. They do not know he sick."

"You knew. You told me to go."

The elderly man placed his hand over his heart. "I pray," he said simply, then pointed one finger upward. "He told me."

Running Fawn did not ask any more questions. There was nothing to do but nurse the missionary herself as best she could.

❧   ❧   ❧

Day after day Running Fawn made the trek over the hill to the little wooden cabin. Day after day she took broth from her stewpot. She brought fresh water, gave him cooling drinks, and sponged his fevered body. Gradually he began to gain back his strength. But he was still not able to leave his bed.

One day he surprised her by calling her name as she opened the door.

"Yes," she replied. "I am here."

He turned his head slightly and even managed a bit of a smile. "I am not sure if you are my nurse—or my guardian angel," he quipped as she bent over him to help him with a drink. She did not answer.

When he had finished he lay back on the pillow and took a deep breath. "Perhaps I should explain," he said, his voice still weak but filled with determination.

"You need not explain," said Running Fawn.

"But I would like to," he insisted. He had switched to English. "When I was very ill, I thought I was going to die. In one way, I welcomed it. It was as Paul said, 'To be absent from the body was to be present with the Lord.' I was weary of fighting. I welcomed it.

"But just as I was about to slip away, a presence filled my room. 'Not yet,' He said to me. 'I have more work for you.' I wanted to argue. Then faces began to pass before me. Faces of those from the Reserve who have not accepted the faith. Calls Through The Night led them past me—one by one— and as they went they looked at me and some said, 'Maybe . . . one day I will understand,' and 'Almost I am persuaded.' I finally said, 'All right, Lord, a little longer if it be your will.' So I prayed. Prayed that if I was to stay, God would send someone to help me.

"And then you came. You see. You were His answer to my prayers. My nurse. My guardian angel."

He managed a weak smile and lay back on his pillow, exhausted.

"You must rest," scolded Running Fawn softly, "or I will

174

need to start my nursing all over again."

He smiled at her teasing but he did not protest.

Running Fawn encouraged him to rest while she went for fresh water. She would give him the broth when she returned.

As she walked toward the river her thoughts were in a whirl. She was hearing such strange things. "He told me," said her father, pointing toward the heavens. "Let him pray," said the bitter Crooked Moose. And now she was being told that Man With The Book had prayed, all alone in his room in his desperate hour of need, and she had come. She was not anxious to be the answer to the missionary's prayers.

Yet she could not deny it. She was there. Feeding him. Nursing him back to health again. Could it possibly be that his God—?

Running Fawn switched her thoughts to other things. It was too much for her to untangle.

Chapter Eighteen

Choices

Running Fawn lifted her head at the sound of an approaching horse. It was the pony, Little Giant, ridden by Silver Fox. She felt her heartbeat quicken and dipped her head back to the hide she was tanning.

He ground-tethered the small animal and moved to stand before her. Only a portion of his fringed leggings resting on the tops of his beadless moccasins were in her view.

"I see your hands are busy," he observed in their own tongue.

She looked up then and nodded slightly.

For several moments he stood silently while her long, slim fingers worked at the leather. "You do the tanning well," he said at length.

She laid aside the deer hide and stood to her feet, her shyness seeping away. After all, they had spent many days together on the journey home. She managed to lift her eyes.

"It is a long time since you have graced our fire," she said with just a touch of reproof in her voice.

She could see in his eyes that he acknowledged her rebuke.

"Silver Fox has not done well," he admitted softly.

His words surprised her. She had not expected him to show any embarrassment about his absence. His next words surprised her even more.

"Could you spare a moment for a walk to the river?"

She let her eyes lift to his and saw conflict there. What was bothering Silver Fox?

She turned briefly toward the tepee where her father rested from the afternoon sun. She was sure she would not be needed in the immediate future. She nodded, then began to move slowly toward the path that would take them to the water.

He followed closely, and when the path widened, he moved up to walk by her side.

They did not speak. She knew he had something to say that he considered important, but she did not press or pry. He would speak his mind when he chose to do so.

They reached the river and walked down the grassy slope to stand near the river's edge. Small bushes clung closely to its winding sides, their roots stretching down to draw from the stream's coolness. Birds dipped above the murmuring current, swinging up on tireless wings and dipping again. Running Fawn felt her inner being becoming at one again with nature as it had when she was a child.

It was cooler along the banks. Cool and peaceful. The ripples sang softly as they passed by, even though the water's flow of high summer was rather shallow after the passage of spring's melting snow. And as the stream moved through the parched land, the sun also spent much of its moisture in steady evaporation. Daily the nearby ground soaked up the life-giving water, just as did the deer, the antelope, and the people. Still the water did not fail. Still it continued to give. The river. The source of relief, of sustenance, of life to the prairies.

Silver Fox made a motion with his hand, and Running Fawn eased herself to the soft, cool grass, her ears still full of the laughter of the stream.

"I have much on my heart," the young man began, and Running Fawn knew he felt the time was right to express whatever it was that was on his mind. Silently she waited for him to go on.

"The chief is old," continued the young brave, and Running Fawn acknowledged that fact with a slight nod. She also knew there would be little doubt of Silver Fox being the next chief of the band. Perhaps one day he might even be head chief of the whole Blackfoot tribe. Who was to know?

"I need wisdom to lead my people," Silver Fox continued. He reached down to pick up a small stone and with a quick flick of his wrist sent it skipping across the stream. Three jumps. One skip was the most Running Fawn had ever been able to accomplish—and Silver Fox had not even really tried.

"When Chief Calls Through The Night leaves us, I must be ready."

Running Fawn thought that the young man was already prepared. She had no doubt that, though he was young, he would make a good leader for the people.

"My father says he wants me to go back to the mission school and—"

But Running Fawn turned off his words. She did not wish to hear them. As a young maiden approaching her sixteenth winter, she had hoped that Silver Fox had brought her to the river to speak of other things.

"You will go back?" she interrupted, her voice choked and incredulous.

"I must."

She felt like jumping to her feet and arguing with him. But she did not stir. Instead she spoke slowly, softly, "What if Calls Through The Night does not live until your return?"

"Our good-byes will be spoken."

"What if, in your absence, someone decides to challenge your place as chief?"

"Sam Tall Man will send for me. I will be here for my father's burial."

"And after—? Will you . . . go back to the school after—?"

Running Fawn could not finish the question, but Silver Fox answered simply, "I will stay with my people."

Running Fawn felt a wave of excitement sweep through her. He would be back. He would not stay with the white man to live in the new world that he seemed to think held so much promise. He would return to his people and their ways. Dared she hope that he would also return—to her?

But he was speaking again.

"Your father is much better."

Running Fawn nodded.

"Perhaps Crooked Moose will take a wife soon."

Running Fawn looked up in surprise. She knew nothing of Crooked Moose and his plans. She found him to be moody and uncommunicative, and mostly absent from his father's fire.

"Perhaps he will bury his sorrow," continued Silver Fox.

Running Fawn's dark eyes held many questions.

"You do not know?" asked Silver Fox quietly.

Running Fawn shook her head.

Silver Fox leaned forward slightly and picked at the pebbles near his hand. "You did not know that Crooked Moose was to marry? His future wife had taken the Christian faith. White Cloud wished to be married in the church and the day was set. She wished for Crooked Moose to also take the faith, and he was meeting with Man With The Book to learn of the Scriptures. But White Cloud became sick and soon died."

Why had she not heard? Why had they not told her? She had no idea that Crooked Moose had gone through such sorrow. No wonder he was so cynical. So angry. No wonder he had such intense feeling against the missionary and the church. She shook her head, trying hard to sort through her own troubling thoughts.

"I thought you knew," apologized Silver Fox.

"No—I did not know."

"I am sorry—"

"No—I should have been told. Father . . . says little . . . and Crooked Moose is never home, and when he is he just . . ." She let the words hang. She felt sudden compassion for her brother.

"But you say he—" she began, deliberately pulling her attention back to Silver Fox's other words.

"He may marry?" he said to finish her question. He nodded. "He has been leaving his offerings at the tent of Laughing Loon."

"Laughing Loon?" exclaimed Running Fawn. She could hardly believe that the friend of her childhood might soon be a part of her family.

Then a sobering thought stopped her excitement. Laughing Loon was close to her age. If Laughing Loon was old enough to become a bride, wasn't she, Running Fawn? Her cheeks flushed slightly and she stirred restlessly.

Silver Fox began to speak again. "With your father much better and Crooked Moose soon to bring a wife to his fire, I was wondering—"

Running Fawn's heart began to race.

"—would you consider returning to school to finish your education?"

Disappointment, then anger filled the heart of Running Fawn. She did stand to her feet now, but she did not lash out at the young man who had also risen. As he waited silently for her answer, he seemed totally oblivious to the pain and frustration he had just brought upon her.

When at last she was able to speak, her voice was low and controlled, though edged with an icy chill.

"I will not go back to the mission school of the white man," she said with finality. "I was not happy there. I missed my people. Their ways. Their gods. I was not one of them. Will never be one of them. Their school, their God, their ways, they are for them—not for the Blackfoot. Let them teach their own people. I will live and be buried with mine."

Silence followed. Running Fawn used the time to quiet her troubled spirit, and Silver Fox looked off in the distance, his eyes mirroring deep, troubled thoughts. At last he spoke.

"And if Crooked Moose brings another woman to your father's fire—?"

"Let Crooked Moose build his own fire. Let him raise his own tepee. I will care for my father," she said sternly.

"And who will bring meat for the cooking pot?"

"My father is not a tottery old man. He is still wise in the hunt."

"But you need—"

She swung to look at him, her dark eyes challenging any statement that he might intend to make. "We need no one," she said, her voice full of vehemence.

"Then I—" began Silver Fox, and Running Fawn saw his shoulders sag and heard the disappointment in his voice even as he began.

"Go," she said, turning away from him.

She did not hear his footsteps retreat. Did not see the lithe frame leave her side, but as the silence slowly seeped in against the background of the gentle singing of the flowing stream, she knew that he had gone. She was alone.

❧   ❧   ❧

The days that followed contained great sorrow for Running Fawn. She wondered if she had done the right thing. She added to her pain by picturing how it might have been had things turned out according to her dreams. She longed to turn back the clock in order to give opportunity to plead with Silver Fox to stay—or else to agree to go with him. But there was no way to take back what had already transpired.

She continued her nursing duties. Her father really needed little care. He had improved rapidly over the weeks that she had been home. But the missionary still needed daily provisions and care.

The first few visits had been in accordance with her father's orders, and Running Fawn had resented them, but obeyed. As she saw the grave condition of the young missionary, the journeys to his home became filled with compassion. Now that he was gradually recovering, the daily jaunts with the nourishing food became a welcome break in her otherwise busy but troubling day, and she found herself looking forward to them. The diversion took her thoughts from Silver Fox and his absence and Crooked Moose and his plans. What really would become of her? Would Crooked Moose bring Laughing Loon to his father's tent? Would there be one too many women at the fire?

The day came when she was surprised to find the missionary seated at the table, his Black Book spread out before him. He smiled as he lifted his head to greet her.

"You are up," she said as she entered the small cabin. She stopped to place her small basket on the shelf by the door. "Are you sure—?"

"I have been in that bed for quite long enough," he replied in English. "If I stay there any longer I will grow attached. I have no desire to become part of it—so I am up. And I plan to be up each day from now on."

She smiled, pleased that he had improved to such an extent.

As she moved about the room to light the fire and heat his simple meal he continued to speak, "I need to get back to the council fires. The news I am hearing is very disturbing."

Running Fawn raised her eyes. Was he speaking of Silver Fox and his leaving? She had said nothing. Surely it wasn't of Crooked Moose. It was true that Laughing Loon had not accepted the Christian faith as had the other—what had Silver Fox said her name was?—White Cloud, that was it. White Cloud. She had been a Christian—had wished to marry in the church, Silver Fox had said. But Crooked Moose still had not taken the white man's faith. Surely it wouldn't disturb the missionary if he married in keeping with the old traditions of the people?

"Is there much talk around the campfires?" asked the missionary.

"We have few people visit our campfire," Running Fawn replied. "I hear little talk. I have been busy caring for my father."

"Of course," agreed the missionary, slipping back into the tongue of the Blackfoot as easily as he had slipped into the English of his birth. "Two of the elders came at last moon's rising. They spoke of much trouble. A man by the name of Riel is planning a rebellion."

Running Fawn stopped short her meal preparations. Who was Riel—and why would his rebellion affect her people?

"He is a Metis—and is asking his full-blood brothers to join his cause," went on the missionary.

"But why? In what?" asked Running Fawn weakly.

"He is angry with the white settlers. He wishes to drive them from the land. Reclaim it for the Indian people."

"Metis are not Indian," said Running Fawn with a hint of scorn, but at the same time her blood began to pound in her veins. Drive out the white settlers. Reclaim the land. It was an exciting thought and one that carried with it great possibilities of fully returning to the old ways of life.

"No—they are mixed blood—but they are more Indian than white. They have more sympathy for the Indian cause," went on the missionary.

She let the statements go without further challenge.

"So far the chiefs have not given an answer. But they will soon be pressed to make some reply. To stand for one side or the other." He was speaking in English again. He sounded concerned and, yes, tired, as though the thought of what lay ahead weighed heavily upon him.

"Will Calls Through The Night be given a choice?" she asked quietly.

"Yes—all the chiefs will need to make a choice," he answered. "Chief Crowfoot will listen to the counsel of his lesser chiefs."

Chief Crowfoot. Yes. He would be the one to speak for the people. Running Fawn envisioned the great chief as she had seen him on more than one occasion as a child. Majestic. In his movement. His manner. He carried himself proudly, with great dignity, and when he spoke, even the white man listened. She felt deep pride for their chief. Surely he would consider carefully. Would choose wisely. Perhaps the white man would soon be gone from the land. Perhaps there would be no white mission school. Perhaps Silver Fox would soon be back with his people.

But even if all of that happened, what would it mean to her? She had sent him away. She, a young maiden, daring to dismiss the son of the chief. Had her years at the white school cost her dearly? Had she forgotten the ways of her people? Was it already too late to reclaim much of the past? Sorrowfully she turned back to the white missionary.

"What do you think they will decide?" she asked softly.

"The Bloods are already itching for war," he said frankly. "It has been too long since the young braves have spilled blood. They are restless—perhaps bored. They are crying for a chance to become involved in the conflict."

Running Fawn nodded. The Bloods were known for their warring. Life on the Reserve was undoubtedly unexciting compared to their past ways.

"The Bloods are fierce fighters," she agreed, remembering how she had often thanked the Sun God that the Bloods were not her enemies. "They are also a strong nation with many warriors. If they join the Metis—"

"Oh, they are not looking to join the Metis," cut in the missionary. "Bull Shield has asked the Mounties for rifles. He says they will put down the Metis rebellion quickly."

Running Fawn could not believe her ears. Yes, the Metis were not Indian. But they were much closer to being Indian than the whites who had taken the land. Would her people really side with the whites in a conflict? It was hard for her to believe.

"I fear there are going to be some difficult days ahead," said the missionary, his weary shoulders slumping, "and some hard decisions to make. I need to get back to the council fires."

❧   ❧   ❧

The discussions were lively. The Indian bands were restless, agitated, and feeling deprived of what had been their rights. Living on the Reserve was not the same as living on the great plains, even if they had in the past needed to defend their borders and their herds of horses from the attacks of neighboring tribes. There were those who were anxious to put their strength behind the Metis. Drive out the whites. Take back their land.

Cooler heads reasoned. The white lived peaceably. The North West Mounted Police patrolled the land. There had not even been reason to fear attacks from other Indian bands since their coming. The law was to protect everyone, regardless of race or tribe. The government had kept the promise to provide tools, guns, and the medicine chest. True, there had been times when the food supplies had been scant and the medicine chest had been empty, but those in charge had sought to correct the situation and live up to their part of the treaty.

Besides, the buffalo were gone. The animals would no longer supply the food and clothing needed. That meant quite simply that the Indian peoples could no longer care for their own needs. If the white man was driven out, how would they survive?

It was not easy to find the answer. The chiefs thought long and hard, seeking wisdom from their gods for the answer. When the last council fire had been reduced to ashes and the great Chief Crowfoot rose to speak for his people, his answer was unswerving, his voice strong. The Blackfoot Nation would not join the Metis of Louis Riel. They would have no part in the rebellion.

Some of the Crees of the north chose to fight. They had long been enemies of the Blackfoot, so it was a surprise to many when, over the months that followed, renegade Cree families were silently welcomed to Crowfoot's fire and given nourishment from his cooking pot.

He may not have thought it wise to go to war for the land, but neither would he turn his back on those of kindred blood, even if through the long years on the prairies they had, in the past, lived as his enemies.

Chapter Nineteen

Winter

Running Fawn could not have explained why she continued to take the walks down the path that led to the home of the white missionary. Perhaps though she was no longer specifically needed, she still felt some measure of responsibility. Maybe she feared that if she did not feed him properly he would soon be sick again and needing further nursing care. Or it may have been that she was lonely and needing someone to talk to, if only for a few moments. The way of life on the Reserve was not like the old. There was no longer a ring of tepees, each with a fire and busily engaged chatting women. They were scattered over the land that they had been given, and the new kind of life did not suit Running Fawn.

Her father was well enough now to walk to the nearest council meetings and talk with the other older men, but he rarely shared with her the news that circulated through the camp. The fires that he now shared were with those of the other Christians among the people. Running Fawn supposed that they did not talk of the same things that they had spoken of in the old days.

Crooked Moose had taken his Laughing Loon and set up his own tent some distance from where his father and Running Fawn had their dwelling. Laughing Loon wished to be closer to her own family.

Running Fawn often found herself longing for companionship.

If she wondered about the absence of young braves making open declarations of intent, she did not let herself dwell on it. Did the rest of the band know that the chief's son had already left his gift at her door?

She thought of Silver Fox. She could not have denied it. But her thoughts were troubled and confused. What had he meant by his visit? If he was following the custom of their people, why had he left her and gone back to school? What might be his feelings when he returned? Would her one word, "Go," be seen as a final dismissal with no future contact? She had no answers, so she tried to push all of the disturbing thoughts aside and concentrate only on her many tasks and the preparation for the coming winter.

But daily she placed food in the basket and walked the short distance across the browned grasses to call at the missionary's door.

She learned that she must go early. Now that he was feeling much better, he was often up and off to call on one of his little flock or to speak to an, as yet, unyielding prospective convert. He took trips to see various government officials or to the forts of the North West Mounted Police, always presenting the needs or causes of his people. And he also made his appearance at council fires, having been invited by Crowfoot himself.

But before he left each morning, he spent time reading his Black Book and in his manner of praying. Running Fawn knew that. He also wrote letters and reports. So if she went during the early part of the day, she would catch him still at home.

It was much easier to talk with him now. She had put aside her shyness and become quite at ease with their bit of friendly exchange. He often asked her questions and listened attentively to her answers. For some strange reason, she felt more a *person* in those morning chats with the missionary than at any other time of her day.

"Are your people saying it will be an early winter?" he asked as he watched her lift the day's portion of food from her basket.

"I have not heard them say," she admitted. Her father had not expressed his views on the matter, and she had talked with no one else for several weeks.

"There is to be a religious ceremony soon," he went on. "The people are giving thanks to the Sun God for a good harvest of their crops and gardens and seeking his favor for a mild winter."

She had not heard.

"Where will it be?" she asked.

"In the south camp—near Crooked Hill."

Running Fawn knew the place.

"The Christians will not be attending," went on the missionary. "We will have our own service and seek the blessing of the Holy God."

Running Fawn said nothing.

"Your father will be coming to the church." His words reminded her that she and her father were now traveling different paths. It brought renewed discomfort to her heart.

"Will you join him?" asked Man With The Book.

Running Fawn shook her head. "I could not do that," she said softly. "I have not taken the Christian faith."

"We would still welcome you," he was quick to inform her. "You might learn from the service, and better understand what we believe."

"The Sun God would not be pleased," she cut in quickly. "Already he has been angered by those who have left his fires to turn to the white man's God."

"Running Fawn," the missionary said patiently, pushing back his Black Book and looking at her earnestly. "I have tried to help you understand that the God of heaven, the Creator of all things, the one who sent His Son to die for mankind, is not the *white man's* God. He is the God of all—all people of whatever color or nation."

Running Fawn had heard the words before but she had

not been able to believe them. Wasn't it the white man who came with the new God? The Indians had not known of Him before the missionaries came to the land. Yet they had worshiped for years. Had held to a religion. Wouldn't they have known if they had been wrong?

"I will go with my people," she said stubbornly.

"If winter comes, will you have fuel for the fire?" he asked, instead of pursuing the matter further.

Running Fawn quickly took up the new subject. "The buffalo chips, once so plentiful, are nearly gone. Soon we may need to seek other means of keeping the fires burning."

"I have been speaking with the Agent. Telling him that we are soon going to need wood hauled to the camp," said the missionary. From there the conversation moved easily to other, more ordinary, things.

❧   ❧   ❧

The invitation was repeated. "Would you like to come with me to the church service?" her father asked amiably. Running Fawn hated to be seen as defying her father, but she shook her head slowly.

"I wish to go to the gathering of my people," she responded.

"The people of the meetinghouse are *your* people," he answered, his eyes reflecting his concern.

Running Fawn was not sure what to say in answer, so she let his words pass.

"It is a long way to travel to the meeting place alone," he said, dropping the matter of the church service.

"I will enjoy the walk."

She could have said that she would not go far until there would be others to join. Many would be traveling the distance to the campsite where the religious ceremonies were to be held.

He nodded and did not press her further.

Running Fawn felt some excitement as she prepared for

the journey. It had been a long time since she had taken part in the ceremonies of her people. She hoped that she still remembered the rituals—the words to the chants. She did wish that she had family members to accompany her. For the first time in several months she ached again for the presence of her mother. Her mother would know what to do.

But Running Fawn was determined. Though she might feel uncomfortable in the beginning, she was going to seek out the old ways of her people and become involved again with the religion that had been passed down from generation to generation. And with that purpose in mind she made her preparations.

She could not find an eagle's feather, though she searched through all of the belongings in the tepee. What had happened to the one that had been her mother's? That should now belong to her. There was not even a trace of it or her father's feather. Where had they gone? Surely her father had not departed so far from the old ways that he had disposed of them. The gods would be angry. No wonder their cooking pots were sometimes empty. Running Fawn felt shivers of fear run up her spine. Worse things would be happening in the future, she was sure.

She would go to the ceremony anyway. Perhaps she would be able to trade something she possessed for an eagle's feather. She wished she had thought ahead. She would have made a quest of her own, in search of one. The missing eagle's feather was not a good omen.

It was only the first bad omen of the whole experience. As she traveled toward the gathering place of her people, she noticed many things that made her tremble with fear. Tirelessly she searched for good omens to offset the bad, but could find little to put her mind at ease.

It is as I have feared, her troubled thoughts raced. *My people will be punished for the way they have chosen. Taking the religion of the white man will only add to the anger of the gods.*

190

❧ ❧ ❧

"How was your trip?"

Her father asked the question. Running Fawn looked at him guardedly. He sounded sincere in his query, but she did not answer with any enthusiasm. "It went well."

"Our service went well also," was his reply.

Running Fawn nodded.

The truth was her trip had not gone well at all. In the first place she walked the entire way alone. Any of her people that were moving her direction were either in the distance ahead of her or far behind. That was another bad omen. When she arrived she was not able to procure an eagle's feather. Another bad sign. She joined the crowd of young women but she did not feel that she belonged there. They were her own people, yet she felt like a stranger in their midst.

She remembered the chants—for that she was thankful, but they did not satisfy her inner being as she had hoped they would. In fact, she had arrived empty and had returned empty, in spite of her honest endeavor to take part wholeheartedly.

Her trip home was no better. Again she walked alone. Again she searched the land and the heavens looking for some sign—some indication that their prayers had been heard. That the gods had been pleased by their rituals. But she found nothing that lightened her heart or gave her hope. Secretly she wished she had not gone. She wondered if she would ever find the desire to go again. But her thoughts troubled her. She would not have dared to voice her thoughts and feelings. Surely she would be gravely punished by the gods. Surely only trouble lay ahead.

And winter, the enemy of her people, lay just ahead.

❧ ❧ ❧

She did not return to her custom of taking food to the young missionary. Fear held her back. Fear because her religion no longer brought satisfaction to her soul. Fear because he seemed so content in his. Fear also that her gods, even though they no longer brought her pleasure, might indeed begin to bring her great pain. In her heart she had already deserted them. Or had they deserted her? She was not sure. She only knew that the religion she had hoped to re-embrace now left her empty and unsatisfied.

She was puzzled and lonely, but she did not know where to turn for an answer to the pain within.

The first snow of winter arrived only two days after her return.

It is as I feared, already the gods are venting their anger, she thought silently.

But the storm was not one of fury. The gentle snowflakes fell in soft swirls that turned the ugly brown of the camp to blanketed whiteness, and then stopped as suddenly as it had come. Her father appeared from the shelter of the tepee, smiling, gun in his hand.

"We will have fresh meat for the cooking pot," he said with confidence. "It is good snow for tracking."

True to his word, when he returned he had a fresh kill flung over the back of his mount.

Running Fawn was stirring a pot of savory stew when another horse appeared. It was the missionary. Her pulse quickened with tension. She had not seen him since her return. Her father left the skin he was scraping and moved toward the young man, a broad smile of welcome on his face.

"Sit at our fire," he said with enthusiasm. "We have fresh meat tonight."

Man With The Book dismounted, his nose twitching slightly as the aroma filled the air. "No one makes a pot of stew like Running Fawn," he observed.

Running Fawn flushed at the compliment and bent her head to stir the pot. The man would not need to be encouraged further to join them, she was sure.

The two men seated themselves before the fire and settled in to visit. Most of the talk was about the little group that formed the local church. Wider interests were also discussed. Running Fawn listened with one ear as she dished out generous helpings and handed them to the occupants of the log seats.

"I had a letter from Silver Fox," the man said, not realizing what his simple words would do to the heart of the young woman.

"He has accepted the Christian faith. He had hoped that his father would make the first move, but he said that he could wait no longer. His heart cannot deny that Jesus is the Christ, the Son of the living God."

Running Fawn felt her whole body stiffen. Silver Fox, the chief's son? He had taken Christianity? What would Chief Calls Through The Night think of his son's denial of the people's religion? Would he remove his son from the right to follow him as chief? It would be logical. And expected. And Running Fawn had heard that a nephew was anxious for the honor.

Her father was beaming as he expressed his pleasure at the news. Running Fawn found it hard to understand. Did her father realize the importance of the step that the young man had just taken? Did he know that it might ruin his whole future?

"Does the chief know?" asked her father.

The missionary was nodding his head. "He knows. Silver Fox sent me to talk to him—and to deliver his words in a letter."

"What did the chief say?"

Running Fawn's whole world seemed to come to a standstill as she waited for the answer to the question.

"He said he will give the words much thought," replied the missionary.

Running Fawn felt her knees weaken. *Much thought*. What would that mean? What would the outcome be? Perhaps . . . perhaps Silver Fox would never come back to his people.

✧ ✧ ✧

Running Fawn did not go back to the cabin of the missionary, but he often joined them at their campfire. He was always welcomed by her father and, indeed, if Running Fawn had felt free to express her feelings, she would have welcomed him also.

In spite of the fact that she still did not share his religion, she did enjoy his company. He always brought news which he shared generously. He even drew her gently into the conversation. Her father did not seem to object. In fact, he too seemed to welcome her opinions on topics under discussion.

Winter settled in around them. The wind blew on some days. The snow fell in gentleness or with sweeping blasts—but it was not a bad winter in spite of Running Fawn's fears.

The Riel Rebellion was quickly and efficiently defused without the help of the Blood warriors, and though there were those who secretly felt disappointment at the white man's victory, nothing like that was openly declared. Starvation did not strike the people. Sickness did not sweep through all the tents. Running Fawn began to realize that the bad omens that had gripped her in such fear were not bringing the bad fortune she had imagined.

Perhaps she could breathe more easily. Spring was just around the corner.

Chapter Twenty

Into the Flames

A strange haze lay over the distant hills as Running Fawn picked up her pail and headed to the river for her day's water supply. She was later than normal in making the short journey, but she did not mind. She had spent the morning chatting with the missionary, who had made his daily call in the early hours of the day rather than his customary evening visit. Now he had gone, and Running Fawn was left to hurry with the tasks that had been delayed.

As she walked, her thoughts were on other matters than filling the bucket in her hand. She now enjoyed her times spent with the missionary. She had almost ceased to think of him as white. He seemed to be more akin to her than many of her own people.

Her people. She should be making more effort to keep contact with her brother, Crooked Moose, and his wife. She would not even have known that Laughing Loon was with child had not her father come bearing the exciting news.

She wondered if Crooked Moose had been able to put away his bitterness now that he had a wife and would soon be a father. She had not seen him for many months.

Nor had she heard from Silver Fox. The only word she heard about him came through his letters to Man With The Book. She was sure the missionary did not know that she waited for the return of Silver Fox to determine what her own future might hold.

But even as she considered her situation, she brushed the thoughts aside. She had not ever been sure that Silver Fox had meant what she had thought he might. And what would the situation be now, with Silver Fox a Christian and Running Fawn still tied to the old ways of her people?

Tied? No. She really had given up the old ways too. She had been disappointed. Disillusioned. But even though she no longer took part in the medicine dances or the religious ceremonies, she was not ready to embrace another religion.

Man With The Book had spoken to her again. Would she not reconsider? He prayed nightly for her salvation. He longed for her to accept his faith. He wished with all his heart, his being, that she might learn to know his God. If only he could make her understand. If she would embrace his faith, then he would be free to . . .

And then he closed his lips tightly and looked agitated and embarrassed. What had he been about to say? Running Fawn's heart raced as she remembered the look on his face. The pleading in his eyes. She did not know the ways of the white man's courting, of making a promise, but she read something in the missionary's eyes that made her cheeks grow warm.

She cast another glance toward the sky. The haze had thickened. She lifted her head and sniffed. Smoke.

Running Fawn was used to the smell of smoke in the air, but this was not the smoke of many campfires. There was a different smell. Acrid. Potent. Grass. Burning grass. She was sure of it. A prairie fire was moving their way.

She turned and raised a hand to shade her eyes. From what direction was it coming? The train tracks? Another spark from the train's steel wheels that had started the dry grasses ablaze?

The fire seemed to be off to the west. She could not see over the next rise to judge the distance. Surely there would be those out fighting it even now. The people who lived beyond the hills were used to the train fires. They would be ready.

She quickened her pace. She must get her water and hurry home. With a fire just beyond the hills, should her father return and find her missing, he would worry.

The river was shallow at the edge, so she waded out into the stream and dipped her pail where the water ran deeper. Lifting the pail with both hands she shifted it to her right hip and walked back to the shore.

The wind had quickened, she noticed, as she took to the trail. That would not help the cause of the fire fighters. She hoped they soon had the blaze under control.

Again she lifted her eyes to the horizon and noticed that the smoke already was much more dense. She was sure that the fire had moved much closer. Panic seized her. Had the fire moved into the area where Crooked Moose and Laughing Loon had their tepee?

She began to run.

There was nothing she would be able to do to save them, but perhaps the missionary could ride for help. She must go to his cabin with all haste.

She had not gone far when she realized that the pail of water hampered her progress. Without a moment's hesitation she tossed it aside, hoisted her buckskin skirts, and ran full stride. She had done well in the school's track events. Surely that would stand her in good stead now.

By the time she reached the cabin, she could see the first flames licking at the dry grasses of the nearby hills. Her eyes turned to search out the missionary's corral fence. There was no horse in the enclosure. She continued on to the cabin anyway, calling out as she ran, "Fire. Fire. There is fire. We must get help!"

The cabin was empty.

Perhaps he is at the church, she reasoned and turned to run on to the small wooden building. There was no one there. Had he gone to another destination rather than returning home?

Gasping from her long run, she turned to stare at the approaching flames. The smoke was thicker now. There was nothing but grass between her and the quickly approaching blaze.

I must get back to the river, she told herself in panic. But even as she spoke the words she knew she would never make the river. There was not time.

For one frantic minute she stood and trembled. She was trapped. Trapped on the prairie with only wooden structures in which to hide and a prairie fire, whipped by the wind, drawing closer with each second.

Her eyes cast about for some way of escape. There was no use trying to run. She would be overtaken before she was beyond the first knoll.

Had she known how to pray, she would have prayed. She did not cry. Common sense told her that she needed to think. More clearly than she had ever thought before.

Her eyes swept the scene before her again—and then they lit upon her only hope of escape. The cistern.

It was not deep. She had drawn water from it many times. But should it be full, the water would be over her head. She had never learned to swim. Even if she was able to hang on to something, there would not be enough room for life-giving air if the water was anywhere near the top.

But it was her only hope. She ran toward it, hoping that the rope was there. At least that might give her something to cling to if the cistern was filled with water.

She managed to remove the heavy wooden cover, though desperation made her hands clumsy. The smoke was now so dense around her that she coughed as she struggled to pull the lid from the well. She groped for the twined rope. She could see nothing.

Ah. The rope. She grasped it tightly and swung herself over the edge. Her feet did not touch water. There would be room for air at the top.

She pushed off, hanging on to the rope with both hands,

sliding down, down, and then the splash as she eventually reached water level.

She expected to sink until she was totally submerged. She clung more tightly to the rope in her hands. To her surprise she stopped short immediately after her feet had felt the cool water. She landed on the bottom in an awkward heap. As she pushed herself up to a sitting position, she found that the water was only a foot or so deep.

With relief she leaned back against the cold concrete and sucked in great draughts of air.

Above her the fire raged. She could hear the crackling of timbers as the small cabin was engulfed, then hungrily devoured. *Man With The Book*, she cried in the darkness, *his home will be gone*. And the church. The little church that he had worked so hard to build. The place where he met with others to worship his God. It would be gone as well. Why? Why had not his God protected it? Why must everything he had worked for be destroyed? It did not seem fair. Perhaps her people deserved punishment. They had deserted their ways, their gods, but the missionary had stayed firm and true. He had allowed nothing to sway him from the path he had taken. Why should his work all be lost?

Running Fawn buried her head in her arms and wept.

☙ ☙ ☙

It was a strange sensation. The wetness of her sitting position seemed to be creeping up her body and pouring in on her head. But that was ridiculous. She knew that. Yet she could not deny the cold moisture that suddenly was wetting her hair and running down the sides of her cheeks. Surely her tears . . . No. Her tears had been warm. This was cold water. She turned her face upward. It was pouring rain.

Rain. With relief she leaned back against the cold concrete and shut her eyes. The rain would do nothing to ease her discomfort, but if it rained hard enough, for long enough, it would stop the advance of the hungry flames. If only it had come sooner. If only the missionary could have been spared.

꜆ ꜆ ꜆

Throughout the darkened hours she sat in the cool water, the prairie night seeming to send long, cold fingers down to the depths of the concrete cistern. She had long since quit her shivering. She was too cold to even feel the chill. Overhead there was still an occasional snap or crackle. Running Fawn guessed that the nearby cabin was still smoldering in spite of the rain that had passed.

Some smoke had seeped into the cistern, making her have occasional fits of coughing, but the strong wind had blown most of it in its wake. She really was quite unharmed. She had never climbed a rope before and was reluctant to attempt the concrete walls in the dark now.

She worried about her people. Her father. Crooked Moose and his expectant wife. Had they survived? She wondered where the missionary had been. Was he at the home of one of his parishioners? The Agent's? Had he ridden to the fort? She hoped that wherever he was, he had not been caught in the path of the fire. She hated to think what awaited him at his return. Everything lost. Everything.

Later, it rained again. But rather than a wind-driven angry rain, this one was gentle. She even welcomed it as it fell upon her head and shoulders.

With the rain, the final crackling stopped. The smoke lessened. Looking up, Running Fawn thought that she might see traces of daylight through the still-heavy haze. It was time to leave the cistern.

With difficulty she pulled herself to her feet. The water sloshed about her legs. Her sodden buckskins felt weighted. She moved about cautiously, flexing aching muscles, working protesting limbs. When she felt that she was ready, she grasped tightly the strand of slippery rope and pulled it taut.

She braced herself and placed one wet foot against the side of the cistern. With the strength of her arms and upward motion of her feet, she began to propel herself slowly up the concrete side. It was working. It was difficult, but it was working. If she could just keep going, she would reach the top and be out in the open again.

Her tight body ached with each forced upward step. Her shoulders pained with the strain. The rope bit into the flesh of her hands with each inch.

She was almost to the top when she heard a sickening rending sound above her head and felt herself dropping through the air. With a splash she landed back in the water, a sharp pain searing through her ankle and shooting up her leg.

She was back where she had started. Only this time a broken rope dangled uselessly in her hands, and her ankle throbbed with pain from her fall. She would never get out now. Never. And no one knew where she was. No one would even think to look for her at the burned-out church site.

❧   ❧   ❧

Even as panic gripped her, something deep inside told her not to give in to her circumstance. To struggle. To fight for survival. *Dig your fingers in and climb*, said the screaming inner voice. *Climb. You must escape. You must. Climb—or you will die.*

With great self-control she stilled the voices. Climb? She could not climb the concrete. Struggle? It would accomplish nothing but to wear her out. Fight? Yes, she would fight— but she must do it by her wits, not her strength.

She carefully drew herself to a sitting position, her painful ankle throbbing even in that motion. *At least the cool water should help the swelling and the pain*, she thought.

Think, she commanded herself as the wave of nausea from the pain gradually receded. *Think.*

What does one need to survive? Her early teaching served her well. Her father had reviewed the lesson with her and her siblings often when they were children.

Fresh air. She had plenty of that. With the top off the cistern she should not run out of an air supply. Still, she reminded herself that every now and then she should wave her arms just to keep the air circulating in the tank.

Water. She had that. She smiled wryly at the thought. This was the first she had ever sat in her water before drinking it. The thought both amused and repulsed her. But the water in the cistern did provide one of her most basic needs.

Food. There was no food. But the human body could survive for many days on water alone.

Warmth. It was cold in the cistern but not dangerously so. Only uncomfortable. And if the sun began to beat down again, it might warm up considerably during the day, even though it would certainly cool off in the night.

One more, she told herself. *I know there is one more. Wits. That's it.* Her father had said one must keep one's wits. Be able to think. Reason. Wits could be the most important factor of all. People with sufficient air had suffocated because of panic. People with water near had been known to die of thirst, people with a food supply at their fingertips had starved. Yes, she had to keep calm. Think. She must not allow herself to panic.

She felt better knowing that even though she was totally helpless, she could survive for some days in her present circumstance—providing she kept calm.

She remembered her flight from the mission school. Ignoring her capacity for reason had nearly cost her her life. She had disregarded the rules of her people and had not made sure she kept aware of the basic needs of her body. In her determination to return home as quickly as possible, her common sense had been depleted by the hot sun and lack of water. She had wandered aimlessly, not being able to think or to act rationally. She could have died on the open prairie. Her fault had been her haste. Her lack of patience.

Well, she would not be impatient now. She would not tire her body with senseless efforts. She would relax and wait for someone to come. Eventually someone would. She would listen for steps, for hoof beats. She would save her energy to call out for help at the proper moment.

For now, she would force herself to relax.

She leaned against the concrete behind her and told herself to think back—back—back—to when she was but a child and had stood in the forests, the song of the gurgling spring filling her ears and the coldness of the granite rock feeling cool and strong at her back.

Chapter Twenty-one

Release

It was a long time before Running Fawn was able to relax enough to sleep. When she awoke her body ached with cramped muscles, tightened by both her slumped position and the cold water. She struggled to her feet, the sudden shooting pain in her ankle reminding her vividly of her recent fall.

Bracing herself against the cold concrete, she began to work her limbs. First her stiff neck and shoulders, then her arms and upper body. There was little that she could do about her legs. The one hurt too much to move and the other was needed to support her upright position.

She lifted her head to peer upward. The sun was gone. Above her, stars sprinkled the evening sky. From her vantage point she could pick out two that were familiar. Her people had often used them as guides in their travels from site to site.

She missed the travels. She especially missed their winter camp. She had loved the mountains. Their coolness. Their freshness. The song of the birds. The ripple of the stream. The closeness of the towering pines and spruce. She missed it all.

She missed her mother. The woman whose efficient hands were always at work over the fire or dressing the hides, providing for her needs and her safe-keeping. The woman whose dark eyes held gentle smiles and genuine care for her. She missed her mother.

In the stillness of the prairie night, with the dim stars way above her head and her body aching from the dampness, Running Fawn lowered herself to her watery seat and wept once again.

ᡃᠯᡃ ᡃᠯᡃ ᡃᠯᡃ

With the coming of a new day Running Fawn scooped up a handful of water and lifted it to her lips. She had to drink, even if she did not welcome the source. Her body needed the moisture, even though she felt sodden from the outside in.

It looked like it would be a bright, warm day. Running Fawn tried to get her thoughts organized for what lay ahead. Above all, she needed to stay alert. Someone might come to the burned-out site. She had to be listening for the sound of steps, ready to call out when she heard any stirring. Once the damage had been surveyed, maybe no one would come again.

All through the hours of the morning she strained for sound. A meadowlark sang nearby. Running Fawn wondered if he was mourning the loss of his nest—calling for his mate. But there was no answering call.

She heard a hawk. She saw him high in the sky, circling, circling, and she imagined his bright eyes alert to movement of any little creature on the ground. She wondered why he didn't move on. Surely he knew that all life of any small prey had already been taken.

Other than the bird life there was total silence. All through the morning hours and on into the afternoon.

The sun moved on, its rays reaching the side of the concrete above her head. She wished she could stretch up. Could lift herself so that the warmth would fall on her back, her shoulders, her aching limbs. She watched as the bright spot shifted, faded, and then was gone.

Again she drank, cupping her hands to hold the wetness,

lifting the moisture to her mouth and feeling it drip off the end of her chin. Again and again she dipped her hands and held them to her lips. It was not like drinking from a fresh mountain stream. The water tasted—of what? She was not sure. Staleness? Her buckskins? She tossed the last cupped handful aside. She had taken enough. It was not pleasing.

Gradually the brightness faded from the sky. A coyote announced the close of another day. In the distance another answered. A low, baying, full-throated call. It sounded mournful on the still evening air. Silently she wished them well on their hunt. They undoubtedly had a den of cubs that needed feeding.

She felt weary, but she was not sure if her discomfort would allow her rest. *I must sleep*, she told herself. *If I do not sleep during the night, I will be drowsy during the warmth of the day and might miss someone's coming*. She made herself as comfortable as she could up against the concrete structure at her back and tried to close her eyes. But sleep did not come.

The stars appeared. Bright and flickering in the sky. An owl cried out in the night, causing her to shiver. She remembered the story of her people. If the owl called your name, it meant that death was near. Had the owl spoken her name in its crying? She shivered again. She did not wish to die. She longed for light and warmth and people. All that gave meaning to living. And if not living, then she longed for peace and consolation in dying. She was not ready to die. Not with her heaviness of heart. She had forsaken the old ways of her people. She had denied her gods. Were she to meet them now, they would not be pleased with what she had become. Should she try to make amends? Was there a way to get back in their good graces? She did not know. The ceremonies. The rituals. They could not be performed in the bottom of a well. She had no eagle's feather. No ceremonial shawl. Nothing. Nothing. But what if . . . what if it was as the missionary said? What if it was as her father now believed? And Silver Fox? What if the Christian's God was the one whom she must face after death? If only she knew. If only she had some sign. Some omen. But the missionary said that the omens of her people were to be disregarded. How then did his God speak? Through the Black Book. But she had no Black Book. Through a silent message to the soul of man, he had said. To the heart. You will know in your heart, he had assured her. It will be stilled, comforted. It no longer will cry for peace. It will be calm, like the loon chick riding securely on its mother's back through the waves of the storm.

Did it really work so simply—so well? She wished she knew. She longed for inner peace. You need to pray, the chaplain of the mission school had informed them. God will hear your prayer.

She wished that she knew how to pray. For the first time in her young life she felt that she would be willing to call out to the Christian God.

❧   ❧   ❧

When the third day dawned, Running Fawn felt so cramped that it was difficult to pull her body to an upright position. Her injured ankle was so stiff and swollen that she could not even force it into motion.

Again she went through her little routine of loosening the muscles of her neck and shoulders, arms and torso. Again she forced herself to drink of the water. Again she lifted her eyes upward, judging the time of day by the position of the sun. She must be alert. She must be ready.

Hour after hour the sun shifted its overhead position. Hour after hour Running Fawn lifted her head, watching the slow movement of the rays on the side of the concrete above her. Midday. Afternoon. Soon the sun would be sinking back to relax in the arms of the distant hills after another long, heat-giving journey.

Her heart felt as heavy as her drenched buckskins. She was about to give up and settle herself for another cold night alone when she felt she heard a stirring. Somewhere out there in the open, something was moving about.

Perhaps it was a deer or an antelope that had come looking for water. Maybe it was a coyote sniffing through the ruins of the cabin. But she was sure that she had heard something.

Quickly she pulled her uncooperative body to an upright position, tilted back her head and cried, "Help," as loudly as she could. There was no response.

"Help," she cried again. The one word echoed back at her, bouncing off the concrete walls.

She listened. Still no footsteps to indicate that anyone had heard and was moving toward the cistern.

She mustered all her strength, braced herself against the concrete structure, and called again. "Help."

Silence.

It must have been an animal, she concluded, deeply disappointed. Her voice had frightened it away.

She slumped back down into a sitting position, her back against the coolness. She could no longer make herself pretend that the firmness that pressed against her was the cool granite stone of the mountain camp.

From overhead a voice called down, its loudness in the silence startling her, "Halloo. Anybody there?"

She jerked upright, her head tilting back to see who was above her, bumping hard against the concrete. "Yes," she cried before the person could move away. "Yes—I am down here."

There was some surprised murmuring. Running Fawn heard English words. Then there was a loud shout. "Parson. Parson—I found the girl. She's down here. The cistern."

Running Fawn sank back into the water. They had come. She was saved. She laid her head on the arms across her pulled-up knees and let all of her pent-up emotions escape in quiet sobs.

♦   ♦   ♦

"Running Fawn. Are you all right?"

Running Fawn recognized the voice of Reverend Forbes. She willed herself to stop her trembling, to wipe away the trace of her tears. "I am well," she called back with a faltering voice.

"Thank God," came the intense response.

There was some anxious discussion, then he called again. "We will throw down a rope. Can you manage it?"

"I . . . I think so," she responded, her voice trembling. More discussion.

"I am coming down," called the missionary. "Stand aside." Running Fawn looked around her. The cistern was not very wide across. Where was she to move to be out of his way?

She managed to get back to her feet just as the missionary lifted his body over the rim of the cistern and began his descent. Running Fawn pushed herself flat against the concrete wall. She could not get her right leg to cooperate at all, so she had to shuffle her weight around.

He landed with a splash beside her and reached out an anxious hand.

"I had about given up," he said huskily as he pulled her to him and pressed her head to his shoulder. "We searched everywhere—day and night. The people from the Reserve—neighboring farmers and ranchers. All of us. We thought . . . I was afraid—I . . . I have never prayed so hard in my entire life."

Up above, a hoarse voice called down, "Ya got 'er?"

Reverend Forbes released her, for the first time seeming to realize his actions. "Yes," he called up, "she is here. She is fine."

"Get the ropes fixed and give us a holler. We'll bring ya up."

Man With The Book turned to Running Fawn, held her gently at arm's length. "I'll send you up first," he told her and proceeded to tie a large loop in the rope.

"I am . . . I am afraid I cannot move . . . well," she shivered. "I—seem to have hurt my ankle."

Immediately he dropped down on a knee as his fingers gently sought out the injury. "It's badly swollen," he stated, his voice showing deep concern.

"Yes," agreed Running Fawn.

"Can you stand the pain? The lift?"

"I think so."

"Perhaps I should hold you."

"No," quickly said Running Fawn, who was already trembling from her last experience of being unexpectedly held. "I will be fine."

He slipped the loop over her head, and she positioned it so that she could sit in the rope.

"Use your hands," he cautioned. "Use your hands to keep from scraping against the sides."

She did not tell him that her whole body was so stiff from the confinement and the cold that she wasn't sure any part of her would function properly, but she clasped the rope with one hand, clinging for dear life, and kept the other hand free to direct her way back to the surface.

She was bumped and juggled as she was hoisted up, but she felt that the additional bruises would not add much to her pain. At last she was seized by outstretched hands and gently eased over the side of the cistern and deposited on the charred prairie sod.

Hands lifted the rope from around her. She did not even look up to see whose faces were bending over her. She was conscious only of the fact that she was free. Free. Safe. The sun in the western sky was just dipping behind the distant hills. Off toward the river a coyote bayed. Another answered. And then the owl called again.

You were wrong—this time, Running Fawn whispered inwardly. *I did not die. You were wrong.*

In spite of her discomfort, she smiled softly to herself as she thrust a hand deeply into the warmth of the blackened soil beneath her.

❧   ❧   ❧

"I am so sorry," whispered Running Fawn when the missionary knelt beside her on the ground. "Your home—the church—everything—gone."

To her surprise he laughed. A soft yet joyous laugh.

"Not quite everything," he said happily. "Look."

Running Fawn turned to follow his pointing finger. There, to her amazement, stood the little church. The charred trail of the fire ran directly up to its door—and then stopped.

"But I thought—" began Running Fawn.

"We were all afraid that it would be burned. During the fire, the Christians got together and prayed and prayed—until the rain came."

Her eyes widened. "You do rain ceremonies?" she asked incredulously.

He really laughed then, throwing back his head and letting the sound ring across the prairie. The other men in the search party were busily engaged in building a fire and preparing to cook something in a pot over the flame. They turned to look at him in surprise.

"No," he answered her. "No, our prayers are quite different from rain ceremonies."

"But—"

"God does answer our prayers. He did. See. There is the answer."

Running Fawn could not argue against the evidence before her. The little church was still standing.

"That was not all we prayed for," he went on solemnly, softly.

She looked at him, her dark eyes soft in the gathering twilight.

"I was afraid we had lost you. We found your water bucket. Scorched black. There was no sign of you. I was afraid—" He did not finish the words, just looked at her, his eyes intense, his lips trembling. Running Fawn lowered her gaze. She did not understand the message that he seemed to be sending her.

Chapter Twenty-two

Chief Calls Through The Night

The fire had been confined to a rather narrow strip across the Reserve. Its reign of terror had been shortened by the soaking rain riding in on the wind. Seven campsites had been lost to the flames, and to the sorrow of the residents, one elderly woman had died from the smoke and a child had sustained burns. It was not good news, but it could have been much worse. Running Fawn was relieved to discover that her father was safe, as were Crooked Moose and Laughing Loon, though the expected child had arrived prematurely.

They named the little girl Born Too Soon and nursed her with great tenderness. Running Fawn was not recovered enough from her ordeal to make the short journey to see her, so as soon as they deemed the baby strong enough to travel, they brought her to the camp of her grandfather, Gray Hawk, and her aunt Running Fawn.

The grandfather was allowed the first peek. He took the baby gingerly, but then his arms circled her as though to protect her from all earth's evils.

"We have come for your blessing, Father," spoke Crooked Moose.

Gray Hawk lifted eyes full of light. "And I shall happily give it." Then he looked down at the infant sleeping in his arms and spoke softly. "At last I have a blessing worthy to give, not in the old tradition of our people. It is the blessing of a mighty God."

He looked up into the eyes of the son who towered above him. Running Fawn knew he was asking for permission to break with the old.

Crooked Moose said nothing but exchanged glances with his wife. At last he turned back to his father and gave a short nod.

With a hand on the head of the infant, the man lifted his voice in blessing, speaking in his own tongue. Running Fawn felt that she had never heard his voice so strong. So sure.

"The Lord bless you and keep you. The Lord make His face to shine upon you. And be gracious unto you. The Lord lift up His countenance upon you, and give you peace. Amen."

There was silence following the prayer.

Running Fawn saw Crooked Moose swallow and then shift his weight to his other foot. He seemed uncomfortable with his deep emotion. "So—little sister," he asked in a louder voice than necessary, "do you wish to greet your new niece?"

Born Too Soon was gently taken from her grandfather and carried to her aunt Running Fawn.

Reclining on a heavy robe, her bound ankle stretched straight before her, Running Fawn smiled as the small bundle was placed in her arms. "What a beautiful baby," she said with deep feeling.

Crooked Moose smiled his pleasure and Running Fawn hoped that the coming of the child had erased the final bitterness from his heart.

"She looks like Mother," she said, glancing up at her older brother.

He nodded. "It is as I said," he responded.

Laughing Loon only smiled softly. Let them exclaim over my baby, her expression said. It was a good omen for the father's family to claim family resemblance, connection, with the child.

"She is so tiny," exclaimed Running Fawn as she fingered the dainty hand.

"She is strong," put in the father with pride.

All eyes lifted at the sound of an approaching horse. Running Fawn recognized immediately the brown gelding of the missionary. She held her breath. How was her brother going to react to a visit from the reverend?

But Crooked Moose, though not enthusiastic in his welcome, was courteous. Nor did he refuse to share a cup of the coffee that Man With The Book prepared over the open fire.

"One good thing the white man brought us," he even joked as he raised his cup. The white man at the fire laughed good-naturedly.

When the coffeepot was empty, Crooked Moose and Laughing Loon bundled their baby back in her cradle board and prepared to leave. The missionary stepped forward just before they mounted their ponies.

"We would be happy to have you bring your new daughter when she is old enough for Christian training," he said without hesitation or apology.

Running Fawn wished he had not spoken so directly. It had been an amiable visit. Surely he should not push so soon. She saw a frown crease her brother's forehead.

But it was Laughing Loon who spoke. "We have been talking," she said forthrightly. "We will decide soon."

The pastor offered his hand to one, then the other, a smile lighting his face.

He said no more.

❧   ❧   ❧

"Chief Calls Through The Night is not well," her father said as he entered the tent where she sat on her buffalo robes. Running Fawn raised her head from her beadwork.

"How ill?" she wondered aloud.

"The medicine from the white man's chest does not seem to work," replied her father.

"They have tried the white man's medicine?" Running Fawn was surprised.

"They have tried."

Running Fawn laid aside her handwork and pushed herself into a more upright position.

"Have they tried the medicine of the people?" she asked directly.

He sighed. "They tried," he answered. "First."

"And neither has helped?"

"Neither."

Gray Hawk lowered himself to a robe across the fire pit from her. It was a warm day. There was no need for an inside fire. He sat staring into the cold ashes from fires of the past. Running Fawn felt that she must speak. Her father had been a friend of the chief for many years. They had traveled many trails together. Had sat around many council fires.

"The chief is old," she said as gently as she could. "Perhaps he wishes to make his final journey."

Gray Hawk raised his eyes. "The chief is not ready for the last journey," he said with great sorrow. "He still clings to the past. He has not bowed his proud heart before Almighty God."

The words cut Running Fawn to the quick. She had given little thought to the Christian God since her release from the watery pit that she feared would be her grave. Several times Man With The Book had pressed her to think carefully regarding her future—her faith—but she had managed to put him off, saying that as soon as her ankle was recovered she would think about attending the little church.

Running Fawn reached for her beadwork again. She needed to fill her trembling hands.

"Perhaps . . . perhaps the . . . the Christian God will give him . . . another chance," she replied, her voice a bit shaky. "They say He is a God of mercy."

Her father nodded his head in acknowledgment of her

words. "But His mercy will not last forever," he responded, and a new sadness had entered his voice.

❧   ❧   ❧

Silver Fox did not wait for word that his father had died. As soon as news came that his father was ill, he made haste to return to the Reserve. Running Fawn heard of his arrival from Man With The Book when he dropped by for his daily check on "his patient."

Running Fawn knew the missionary had no idea of the conflict in her heart at the announcement that Silver Fox was back. She hoped her eyes did not give her away as she quickly bent over the fire to add more fuel.

"I have no idea how soon he plans to return to the mission," the missionary added.

"He will not go back," Running Fawn said quietly before she thought to check herself. Her face warmed at her own words. She hoped the missionary would blame it on the heat of the flame.

"What do you mean? Have you talked with him?"

"No. No—not since—his return," Running Fawn floundered. "I—he is to be chief. He will not hold his—duties lightly."

She did not add that Silver Fox had already given his word—and Silver Fox did not give his word lightly either.

The missionary seemed to be pondering her statement. "Perhaps," he said at last. "Perhaps you are right."

Running Fawn changed the subject. "How is the chief?"

"Not well. It is a wonder that he has held on as long as he has. They are saying he is calling for a council fire. Perhaps—like you say—he wishes to name Silver Fox as his successor."

They were right back to Silver Fox again.

"Perhaps," said Running Fawn as she threw another buffalo chip on the fire and turned to the man before her. Her face was flushed, her thoughts confused, but she had no de-

sire to speak further of Silver Fox. "It is becoming harder and
harder to find enough fuel for the fires," she said in English,
surprising even herself. "The buffalo are gone and soon all
of the chips that they have left behind will be gone also. What
are we to do then?"

Her unusual vehemence seemed to surprise and amuse
the man by her fire. After his initial look of shock he began
to chuckle softly. "Give me your baskets," he offered good-
naturedly, "and I will go gather you some. I am sure it is not
easy to hobble out after buffalo chips when you need the aid
of a cane."

Running Fawn did not argue. She retrieved the baskets,
thrust them into his hands, and watched him go.

At least it had not been an untruth. It *was* harder and
harder to find fuel for her fire. It was also the only thing that
she could think of to get the missionary away from her campfire while she tried to sort out her troubled thoughts.

❧   ❧   ❧

Dear Brethren,

Much has been happening on our Reserve. As I have
explained in the past, each Indian nation is comprised
of tribes, and each tribe is made up of smaller bands.
The Blackfoot band that I have chosen to work with has
been until recently under the leadership of Calls
Through The Night, a wise and noble chief. He lived to
an old age—exactly how old, even he did not know. He
lost his first two families in one raid or another and
some of his third family through sickness. However, he
does have a son of his old age. I have written of him
before. The young man was one of the first children to
attend my classes. He then went away to mission
school in Fort Calgary, and except for a brief time home
a year ago last spring, he has been at the school ever
since.

He is a good student. All reports from the school
have been commendable.

He knew when he left the last time that his father was growing old. His father wanted him to gain all the knowledge of the white man that he could so he could lead the people wisely into the new life that has been forced upon them.

Through the diligent teaching of the administrators and faculty of the school, he has accepted the Christian faith, for which we praise God.

He was recently called home because of the illness of his father. He did arrive in time for the old chief to call a council meeting. I was privileged to attend.

It is with both sorrow and joy that I report.

I had shared the Gospel with Chief Calls Through The Night many times since my arrival some ten years back. He always showed polite interest, but also found some way to postpone his decision. I have felt that he was the key to winning the entire band.

At the last council meeting, with two warriors supporting him so that he could sit up, he made his final speech. "I am old," he said, "and I go to my fathers.

"Over the years I have listened much to Man With The Book. Perhaps he has the right way. I do not know. I have lived by the old ways. I die by the old ways. It is the way I know.

"Now I come to my last sunrise. My son, Silver Fox, will be your new chief. He is wise in the ways of our people. He also has been schooled in the ways of the white man. He will make a wise chief.

"He has embraced the Christian faith. It has made his heart glad and given him peace. I want you, my people, to follow him in this way if your heart tells you it is right. Listen carefully to your heart. Once you take the new faith, do not turn back. The Christian God is a jealous God. If you serve Him, you must serve Him only, with your whole heart. Man With The Book has told me so.

"I tire. I am old and long for rest. I will hear the call of the meadowlark no more. The deer will not fall by my arrow, nor the bear fear my approach. I am old.

There is but one more journey for me to take. My heart is anxious to be walking that trail."

And saying his words he motioned for us all to leave. He did not even live to see the morning sunrise.

In spite of Silver Fox's desire to have a Christian funeral, he allowed the people to mourn the chief in the traditional way. After all, his father had not converted to Christianity. That fact saddened the young man, just as it saddened me. If only the man had not been so determined to hold to the old ways.

The time of mourning went on for many days. He was a well-liked chief and the people paid him proper homage. All the neighboring chiefs arrived in full regalia. The Blackfoot, the Blood, Peigans, some Sarcee, and even a few Cree showed up at one time or another during the mourning period.

At last things have settled down. The chief has been buried, the days of mourning past, and things on the Reserve are gradually returning to normal. I am excited about the future. With Silver Fox, a convert from our own mission, now leading the people, I pray that there might be a further turning of the band to the Christian faith.

I have one question that has been awaiting an answer for some time. What is the position of the Mission Society on marriage between races? Do the same rules apply to the clergy as to the laity? I look forward to your answer.

May God continue to bless your endeavors in leadership.

Yours in His service,
Martin D. Forbes,
Minister of Christ.

Chapter Twenty-three

The Book

"I have come to talk."

Running Fawn eased her basket of buffalo chips to the ground and straightened her shoulders. She had expected to have a visit from Silver Fox now that the days of mourning for his father had passed. But the days had turned to weeks, and the weeks to months, and he had not come. She began to think that maybe . . . maybe she had been wrong.

He stood before her now, his face somber, his dark eyes intense. It was strange to see him in full Indian dress. Many of the men on the Reserve had incorporated the cotton shirts and vests of the white man into their own wardrobe. Silver Fox was dressed in buckskin.

She nodded silently, then modestly lowered her gaze.

The day was cool. A north wind had been blowing throughout the night, threatening to bring an early winter to the land. Overhead a flock of Canada geese flapped their way southward, large wings taking advantage of the wind at their backs to conserve some energy for the long journey. They called words of encouragement to one another as they flew, though Running Fawn had always found their honking to be plaintive.

"Do you wish to stay by the fire?" Silver Fox asked, acknowledging the brisk wind and the cool day.

Running Fawn shook her head. Her father had not yet

left the tent. She knew that his aging bones much preferred the warmth to the chill of the wind. She would not disturb him, but he might soon be stirring to check what was in the cooking pot. Instinct told her that this discussion should not be disturbed.

"I will get my heavy shawl," she answered simply.

It was not difficult for her to enter the tent and retrieve her wrap without waking her father. He slept on, his lean body enshrouded in the wool blankets of the Hudson's Bay Company.

The two began a silent walk toward the river. It seemed like the logical place to go. Neither spoke until they reached its banks and settled cross-legged on the grass-covered ground.

"I have wished to come for a long time," began Silver Fox. "I had many duties after my father's death."

Running Fawn nodded, her eyes on the gentle ripple where a submerged rock in the stream almost touched the surface.

"I have not forgotten my promise."

Running Fawn's heart skipped within her, much like the stone that he had thrown into the current when they had visited the stream together in a time that seemed so long ago. She could not keep her eyes from lifting to his. She knew the full implications of that promise. She would be his wife. She knew that it was what she wanted. Had wanted for a very long time. Perhaps ever since the young Silver Fox had guided her carefully, gently, home to the Reserve on the small pony.

"I have not yet paid my debt to the mission," said Running Fawn in a trembling voice. "I gave my word."

The promised payment still hung heavily on her mind. She had worked diligently with her beadwork, but she had no access to a trading post to exchange the work for money.

"The debt is paid," responded Silver Fox simply. Running Fawn did not have to ask who had made the payment.

Silence—for many minutes. Running Fawn stole a glance

at Silver Fox and saw a sober, thoughtful face. Troubling thoughts raced through her mind. Was he regretting the long-ago promise? Would he hold to his word, in spite of his heart? Perhaps . . . perhaps there was another maiden. Maybe even a white girl from the mission school. She did not want to spend her life with a man bound only by a promise. Not if his heart was elsewhere. She wanted . . .

But Silver Fox spoke again.

"I have taken the Christian faith. It warms my heart. It gives me hope for the future. For my people. I cannot lay it aside like a worn moccasin."

Running Fawn nodded silently.

"You cling to the ways of the past," he went on without recrimination. "I am not sure the two ways would go well in the same tepee."

"But I . . . I would not . . . I would understand. You may keep your ways."

Running Fawn had never had such difficulty trying to express her thoughts. Her feelings.

"I do not wish a wife to *allow* me my faith," said Silver Fox seriously. "I desire a wife who *shares* my faith. Who loves my Lord as I do. Who seeks only to follow His way. Who raises our children to understand about His love—and mercy. That is what I want in a home."

Running Fawn's rapidly beating heart seemed to suddenly still. He had come to tell her that he could not keep his promise of old. That they would not be man and wife—ever.

Running Fawn nodded mutely, her eyes cold, her body stiff.

"For that reason I have a request," went on Silver Fox as he reached inside his leather tunic. When he withdrew his hand it held a Black Book. Smaller than the missionary's— yet Running Fawn knew that it was the Bible.

"I ask only that you read its pages," said Silver Fox with intense feeling.

"But I know . . . I already read. At the mission."

"Yes," he acknowledged, "I know that you have heard

many of the stories. I know that you were assigned reading portions. Memorization of passages. You put them from you. Now—I ask one thing. That you read—and that you listen with your heart to the words."

For a moment Running Fawn wished to resist.

"This book is for the white man," she said. "If a Blackfoot accepts the words, his whole life must change."

To her surprise he leaned toward her and took her long, slim hand in his. "Running Fawn," he said earnestly, "*anyone* who accepts the words must change. Any man or woman. White or red. Yellow or black. We may be different on the outside, but inside—" He laid a hand over his heart. "Inside we are all the same. Evil. Sinful. Needing someone to save us from all that. We all need to change our ways—from the inside to the outside."

It was a new idea for Running Fawn.

"Please . . . just . . . just read the book. Promise me," he went on. "Then . . . we will speak again."

So she had not been totally dismissed. There was still a chance. She . . . she . . . Then a new thought struck her and made her swing around to face the young man. Her back stiffened, her eyes flashed. "I will not say that I take the Christian faith just to become your wife," she said, her voice low but full of intensity.

He surprised her with a smile. "I know you will not," he answered evenly. "That is why I dared to ask for your promise to do this—read the Book again."

❧   ❧   ❧

Running Fawn kept her promise. Daily she found time from her duties to spread the Black Book before her and read the English words.

She began with the book of Matthew, and for some reason that she could not explain, it seemed much different to her than when she had read it at the mission school. Then she had seen it as a myth, the white man's way of thinking. Now she was reading it as though the people in the stories had really lived, really shared her world. She often found herself caught up in the pages, forgetting to feed the fire or stir the cooking pot. Her father only smiled.

She read strange words and ideas. A man named John had preached long ago, to white people. He had called them evil and demanded that they repent and put away their sin. *White* people. They had to *accept* Christianity. It was not just naturally theirs because they were white.

The man Jesus, who was also the Son of God, walked by the water's edge and called out to the fisherman. They left their boats, their way of life, to follow Him. Running Fawn was amazed that these white fishermen had been called to change their whole way of living.

On and on she read through the Gospels, and again and again she saw the message, *Let go of the past. Be willing to have your life changed. You need a new life, new ways. What you have clung to in the past will keep you from heaven.* For everyone—and it meant total change. Total submission to God.

But it wasn't until she read the words in the book of Second Corinthians that she realized just how complete that change needed to be. Her eyes widened with surprise and her heart began to race with reverent fear. "Therefore, if any man be in Christ, he is a new creature; old things are passed away; behold, all things are become new." She read the passage in chapter five, verse seventeen, again—and again—emphasizing the words that spoke directly to her heart. "Therefore, if *any man* be in Christ, he is a new creature; *old things* are passed away; behold, *all things* are become new."

If the white man could not have access to heaven without great change, and it was *his* religion, then what hope had the Blackfoot?

No . . . no, that was where her logic was all wrong. Just as Silver Fox had tried to tell her, it was not the white man's religion. Not at all. It was for all people. The verse said *any man*. Those of the Blackfoot Nation had as much right to the salvation offered by the Son of God as any white man.

The thought was both a sobering and exciting one.

Running Fawn read on.

The apostle Paul went about preaching to the people and always his message was the same. You need to repent. You are living in sin. God cannot accept you as His child until you change. You can only change, as God forgives you and changes your heart, through the death and resurrection of Jesus Christ His Son. Then you will change your ways.

"The white people are no different—or better—than the Blackfoot," observed Running Fawn. For a moment she felt a bit of satisfaction from the fact.

But a new, sobering thought quickly followed. They might be no better than the Blackfoot in the eyes of their great God, but neither were they any worse. If they needed to repent, to change their ways, to seek forgiveness and find their way back to God, then so did she, Running Fawn.

With tears in her eyes she turned her attention to the verses that explained how she was to find forgiveness for the evil thoughts and feelings in her heart.

A verse that spoke directly to her was in John chapter three. A new birth. At first it sounded ridiculous. Impossible. No one, once born, could be born again. But as Running Fawn pondered the verses, she soon realized that Christ was not speaking of a physical birth—but a spiritual. Running Fawn had no difficulty relating to the spiritual. Her people had known since their beginning that man was more than a physical being. She was quite willing to accept the fact that she had a spiritual dimension. And yes, she now was even willing to admit that it was not in a proper relationship with a Holy God.

That was the start—a new birth—regardless of one's race. A new birth. God's family was made up, not of a particular nation, but of all those, of any color or race, who had been spiritually born into His family. Running Fawn could easily understand the rights and privileges of birth. Her proud people had handed down those important traditions for generations.

Running Fawn allowed the truth of new birth to fill and illuminate her mind, and she found verse after verse presenting this teaching and explaining how one went about experiencing its reality.

"It is what I need," she finally concluded with tears running down her cheeks. "It is what I have fought against. I need a new birth. Not to change who I am. I have no desire to try to become—white. I will always be Blackfoot. But I have an evil heart. Evil thoughts. I need to be forgiven. To be spiritually reborn. To change on the inside. That is where the change must be. My spiritual being—that inside part that is eternal."

And Running Fawn bent her head and accepted the truths of the Word of God. "If we confess our sin, he is faithful and just to forgive us our sin and to cleanse us from all unrighteousness," she whispered to herself. As she confessed, the tears of sorrow, then of joy, fell unheeded on the hands folded over the pages of the Black Book.

☙ ☙ ☙

Her father did not need to ask what had happened in her life. Her face and manner reflected the joy and peace that filled her heart.

"I think you should visit Man With The Book," he suggested, his face full of his own great joy. "He is planning a baptismal service before the cold of winter comes."

With shining eyes Running Fawn nodded. It was what she wanted. She would speak with the missionary—soon. Baptism would be her first public step of obedience in her new faith.

☙ ☙ ☙

The day was cool but there was no wind blowing. Running

Fawn stood on the shore of the river with the five other new believers and listened carefully to the words spoken by the man standing knee-deep in the frigid stream, his black suit soaking up the water swirling about his legs.

She had been disappointed to learn that Silver Fox would not be in attendance. He had gone to the city on important government business for his people. She had not as yet been able to tell him about her new faith.

At first she wondered if she should postpone her baptism so he could be there. But she had quickly changed her mind. It was important for her to be baptized, and this was the last opportunity before the cold northern winds would move in to lock them in another prairie winter.

"The Holy Scripture admonishes us to 'repent and be baptized,'" said the missionary. "Those of you who stand before me today have repented. You have accepted the work of Jesus Christ on Calvary as your atonement and have asked His forgiveness for your sin. He has accepted you—as He promised. Now you have come to be buried with Him in baptism—to rise again to new life as one of His followers."

Running Fawn felt excitement tingle through her. She was a follower of Jesus. A new spiritual being. A child of God—now fit for heaven through acceptance of His atonement. It filled her with such remarkable joy that she wondered if she would be able to contain it.

Chapter Twenty-four

The Answer

The missionary sat at Running Fawn's campfire enjoying a warm cup of coffee on a chilly autumn evening. He seemed to be deep in thought. Running Fawn could feel his eyes on her as she stitched the moccasin in her hands. She was making sure that her father had proper footwear for the coming winter. The white man's shoes did not keep the winter frost from freezing feet.

Running Fawn felt restless. Her ears were straining for the sound of her father's returning horse, and her eyes pierced the darkness to try to make out an approaching form. He had not yet returned from picking up their allotment at the agency. It was not that she was in need of supplies. It was just that, for some reason, she felt uncomfortable in the present circumstance.

The missionary broke the silence.

"How old are you?"

It seemed a strange question.

"I am past my seventeenth year," she answered and returned to her sewing.

Perhaps he feels that it is strange that a girl my age has not taken her own campfire, she reasoned. Her face flushed slightly.

He chuckled softly, bringing her head up. She had no idea what was amusing to him.

"You have always seemed so mature," he said softly. "I had supposed you were a bit older than that. But looking back—yes, you were merely a child when I first arrived."

He was silent again, then said, "I thought I was quite grown up at nineteen. Imagine." He laughed again—softly and to himself. "Well, I have done some growing up—some aging—since then. Many things have changed."

He shook his head as though sorting through all the difficult years that he had shared with her people.

"So you are seventeen," he continued to muse, staring at the dancing flame of the fire, the cup of coffee forgotten in his hand. "I have just turned thirty. Thirty." He shook his head as though it was hard to believe. Then he looked up and asked candidly, "Do you think that is too old?"

Running Fawn frowned. Too old? Why, her father was much older than that and he still rode in the hunt. Planted the grain.

"No," she said quickly. "Thirty is not too old."

He smiled, then leaned to set aside his coffee cup. "Good," he said and he sounded greatly relieved.

He stood to his full height. He was a tall man. Taller than the Indian people with whom he worked. Running Fawn, sitting on the robe beside the fire, had to look way up to see his face.

He looked serious now. Serious but excited. "I have written the mission," he said, and his usually controlled voice was husky with intensity. "I am awaiting their reply. If they have no objection—and I do hope they will not, I would so much rather be able to stay with the mission—then—"

He stopped and began to pace as though agitated. Running Fawn continued to look at him, a frown creasing her smooth forehead.

He spun around to face her, took a deep breath and continued, slowly, as though he wished her to catch every word.

"Then I plan . . . to ask you to be my wife."

Running Fawn was shocked. Her head reeled, her voice failed her. She wanted to stand to her feet, but she was sure that they would never hold her weight. She looked up at him, then quickly down.

"You may see this as . . . sudden," he went on. "It is not. I have given it much thought. I have prayed . . . and waited. I could not speak until . . . until you had accepted the faith. You will never know the agony of the waiting. The—"

Running Fawn finally rose shakily to her feet. She must speak before he could say more. She held out a hand imploring him to be silent. He seemed to understand her gesture but not her message. He stepped closer and took the trembling hand in his.

"I—you must—I cannot—"

He quickly interrupted. "I know that you must care for your father. We will care for him . . . together."

She shook her head. "No," she said, her eyes begging for his understanding. "No . . . it is not that way. I . . . I am . . . promised."

He looked confused.

"Promised?" For a moment he looked stunned, then he seemed to brighten. "Your father is a Christian now. He would not hold you to the old ways. He would not give you to a man who does not share your faith. He—"

"My father did not make the promise," said Running Fawn quietly, yet with firmness.

"Then who—?"

"Running Fawn," she answered, laying her free hand on her heart.

"You . . . but . . . I do not understand." He looked totally baffled. "When?" he asked her.

"Many years."

"But . . . but how do you know—? What of the . . . the . . . man? Does he expect you to—? Does he share your faith?"

He faltered, then added one more direct question. "Does he still wish to marry?"

Running Fawn withdrew her hand and shook her head in the soft glow of the firelight. Her eyes had softened, her head slowly dipped. "I do not know," she replied in a whisper.

"Then—?" He stepped closer. "Then perhaps . . . perhaps . . . surely, if he has not made his intentions clearly known, then you are free—"

"I do not wish to be free," she said, raising her head and standing tall. "I have decided. If he does not wish to—" for an instant her head lowered again, "—marry . . . then . . . I will stay at my father's fire."

The Reverend Forbes met her eyes and his expression acknowledged that he was seeing the light of a woman in love. He stepped back in recognition that he had no right to this woman. She belonged to another.

"I see," he said softly, and his hands lifted and rubbed together in agitation, then raised to nervously run through his thick brown hair.

He turned back to the fire.

"I am sorry," whispered Running Fawn with sympathy.

All was quiet for many moments. Only the crackling of the fire broke the stillness of the night. Running Fawn wished to speak—wished to make some sort of statement that would ease the pain she saw in the missionary's eyes. But she did not know what to say or how to say it. Not in either of the languages that they shared.

He finally broke the silence. "May I ask who—the man?" he said, his voice still strained.

Running Fawn felt her back straighten as she stood to her full height, her chin up, her head held high. "Silver Fox," she said softly, and there was love and pride in the whispered name.

"Silver Fox?"

Silence again.

"Silver Fox." Then a whispered acknowledgment, "I should have known."

He turned from her and appeared to be studying the brightness of the stars overhead for a very long time. She wondered if he was just thinking—or praying. At last she heard him sigh, then he looked back at her, appearing composed now.

"Silver Fox," he agreed, with a nod of his head. He seemed to have accepted the bitter truth she had revealed.

Running Fawn waited before she spoke again.

"He—if—" she swallowed, finding it hard to continue. "If—then we will want a church wedding," she managed, a hint of question in the comment. Would the missionary be able—and willing—to perform the ceremony?

He nodded. "Of course," he replied.

"Would you rather we traveled to the mission?"

"No. No—it is right that you be married here—on the Reserve."

"I am sorry," she said again.

He turned to her. He even managed a smile. He extended his hand and she accepted it. "I wish you both God's richest blessing," he said sincerely. "I think that you will . . . will make an excellent wife for the new chief. Together you will do much good for your people."

Running Fawn nodded silently. She could feel tears forming in her eyes. In the distance she heard the unmistakable sound of an approaching horse. Her father was finally coming home.

❧   ❧   ❧

And then a few days later, another horse and rider rode up to their campsite.

"I have news," Silver Fox said, and though his voice held excitement, his shoulders drooped. A frown of concern creased Running Fawn's brow. He looked so weary. As though he had been riding for days.

She passed him a cup of coffee, her hand trembling.

"I wished to make the trip to the government offices before the winter storms made travel more difficult," he explained, as though to give answer to the questions racing through her mind. "I am sorry that I have been gone—so long."

She nodded and lowered her head. She was not yet ready

to share the secret she knew would show on her face. She must be patient. Must give him time to warm himself at her fire. To speak of his own news.

She dished out a plate of heated food and turned the bannock in the pan.

"I must not stay long," he apologized. "I should have waited until morning, but I wanted you to be the first to know."

It was hard for her to keep her eyes on the pan.

"Soon you will no longer need to hunt for the buffalo chips."

Her head came up. He sounded so pleased with his announcement.

"I have been to see the government counselors. They will assist in getting the coal mines opened. Soon we will have plenty of fuel for our fires. More than we need for the people. We will even have coal to sell. Perhaps we will not need the government supplies. We will be free to make our own way."

His eyes shone in the firelight. She felt immensely proud of what he had accomplished in such a short time. There had been idle talk about mining the coal for years, but nothing had been done.

She smiled softly. "That is good," she acknowledged.

He lifted his eyes to hers and studied her closely, the fork in his hand forgotten.

"You have read the Book," he said softly. He did not put it as a question.

She nodded, silently, her whole being wanting to shout her news aloud.

He sat, mute and motionless, too moved to speak, the firelight reflecting in his shining eyes.

"I have been baptized," she said in little more than a whisper.

He reached down and set aside his unfinished plate of food. One hand reached out to her, brushing back a wisp of straying black hair. For a long moment he looked into her eyes, sharing her joy, whispering prayers of thankfulness, then he stood, and without a backward glance or a spoken word, he mounted the pony and rode off quickly into the night.

❧   ❧   ❧

The midday sun had picked up a little warmth. Running Fawn made her rambling way over the cold, browned prairie, bending now and then to add another chip to her basket. She found it difficult to concentrate on the simple daily chore. Her thoughts kept returning to Silver Fox.

He had promised that soon she would no longer need to make the daily treks for fuel. She would be burning coal. He had come first to her fire upon his return from the city. He was pleased that she now shared his faith. His eyes had danced. His hand had gently touched her face. She pressed her hand against the very spot, remembering his touch. Holding it to her.

Now if only . . .

But she had to be patient. Had to hold herself in check. There was nothing she could do. It was up to Silver Fox. He would decide if she was indeed to become his wife. The one who shared his campfire. The warmth of his tepee against nature's storms.

But is was so hard to keep her thoughts on what she should be doing. No matter how much she willed her mind to stay with her task, it kept switching back to thoughts of Silver Fox.

"I must build up the fire," she scolded herself. "Perhaps, with God's help, Father will be successful in the hunt today."

Some of her joy momentarily slipped away as she thought of the unsuccessful hunts of late. Yet, they had not gone hungry. As her father continued to declare, God always provided—enough. Enough for the cooking pot. Enough blankets against the chill. Enough hides to dress for new buckskins. Yes, enough. For that Running Fawn was thankful. But on many days, stretching what they had to make it enough was most difficult.

But God would continue to care for their needs, she declared inwardly and her face brightened. Just as she had read in the morning's Scripture passage, "But my God shall supply all your need according to his riches in glory, through Christ Jesus." It was a wonderful promise.

Running Fawn turned her steps and her thoughts toward home. If her father had been blessed with success he may be home soon. She would start the fire.

꙰   ꙰   ꙰

The sound of an approaching rider caught Running Fawn's attention from the small flame she was coaxing into life. Her father was early. That would mean a successful hunt.

But it was not her father's horse that was moving briskly toward the camp. Running Fawn recognized the mount immediately as the pony of Silver Fox.

She lifted herself from her stooped position. Standing perfectly still she raised a hand to shade her eyes against the setting sun. Her heart began to flutter within her. She had not expected him back so soon. She knew the duties of the young chief consumed his days and he would have his exciting report to give to his council. Then there would be much to do to prepare for the opening of the mine.

As he drew nearer she could see that he had a bundle in front of him across his mount, but her curiosity never drew her further. Her thoughts were too busy with the fact that he was coming again to her fire.

Her hand dropped to her side, limp and lifeless, just as she herself seemed to be, except for the rapid pounding of her trembling heart. Had he come to tell her that he had reconsidered—that he was making other arrangements? Was he—?

He dismounted in one easy motion and hoisted the bundle from the back of the pony to his own shoulders. He lowered the robe to the ground and began to unwrap the contents. Running Fawn silently watched the proceedings, willing her heart to begin beating again.

It was fresh venison wrapped in deer-hide that he drew forth from the heavy buffalo skin. Still without speaking, he lifted it up in his arms and moved silently toward her. With his eyes looking deeply into hers he extended the offering. The renewal of his promise of long ago.

She was too moved to speak. Too filled with joy to form words. A small tear trickled down the soft curve of her cheek. She answered the look in his eyes with a steady gaze that did not need to lower in confusion or embarrassment. She understood perfectly well his message. The hint of a smile belied the tear as she reached out her arms to accept his gift. His promise. Their fingers touched briefly as the exchange was made and his eyes held hers. She wondered if she saw a tear glistening in his eyes as well.

And then he turned and was gone, but she did not call to him. Did not worry. She knew that he would soon be back.

With a confident smile she reached up to wipe the tears of joy from her sun-warmed cheek and straightened her back to her fullest height in the way of her people. Her heart sang with the song of the released spring-waters when winter snows were first melted by the strength of the warming sun. Man With The Book would soon be performing a wedding ceremony.